COWBOY AND INDIAN

Darryl Sollerh

COWBOY AND INDIAN
Published by Del Oro Company
ISBN: 978-0-9887254-8-5

COWBOY AND INDIAN

Daybreak gleams over a breath-taking vista of the Silver C Ranch, graced by rolling hills covered in prairie grasses and dotted with shady oaks.

Stirring the crisp morning air, comes the sound of rustling hooves as two cowboys lead fifty head out to pasture.

As the sun arcs higher, Billy, in his able thirties, gallops off to chase down a bolting steer as Ray, a lean late sixties, canters off to coax a calf back to its mother.

Returning their respective charges back to the herd, they trade a knowing glance as they guide the rest of the cows onto a gently sloping hillside to graze.

When the afternoon heat beats down, they pause to munch on beef jerky and peanut butter sandwiches under an oak and then take turns curling up for quick naps, needing only a look to coordinate their routines.

When the sun finally sets in the west, Ray trots up to the crest of the hill to get a better look, admiring the cathedral sky as the herd ambles back to their pen below.

Moments later, Billy rides up alongside and Ray glances over:

That rodeo tomorrow?

Thousand dollar pot.

Ray thinks about it and then shrugs:

Just remember, ya still owe me fifty.

I'll have my accountant write ya a check.

And they trot off into the sunset, heading home.

It's a crowded, dusty day at the local Fair grounds, busy with ranching families lining up for noisy carnival rides, colorful arcade games and deep-fried Twinkies.

The main attraction, a rodeo ring surrounded by temporary bleachers, is brimming with cowboy hats, well-worn leather boots and beers.

As honky-tonk tunes crackle over a public address system, Ray leads Kooch, a sixty-some cowpoke pal with a crew-cut and pronounced paunch, down to their seats:

Front row, Ray?

Wanna be able ta see him, don't ya?

The ring announcer shuts off the music to say:

Next up, folks, we got Billy Wilks from Grand Prairie. Time ta beat is 5.9 seconds, so best of luck there, Billy.

Billy doesn't hear his name over the PA system because he's staring down at the massive, twitching back of an angry bull, only temporarily slowed by the metal-gated chute.

Joe, a seasoned wrangler, straddles the gate over to Billy:

Hey, Billy. How do?

Just another day at the office, Joe.

As Joe helps Billy slide down onto the bull's muscular back, it jerks violently, rattling the rails with its impossible power.

Joe shrugs:

He's been a little moody lately.

Ray and Kooch meanwhile are leaning forward in their seats, squinting as they watch Billy from a distance:

Holy crap, Ray, he drew Wild Child.

Ray looks over as Koch shakes his head:

Moodiest sumbitch bull they got. And that's on a good day.

As Ray looks back at Billy, with increasing concern, Billy, all business now, winds a leather strip around his leather-gloved right hand, securing it to the horn of Wild Child's harness.

He then tucks the end under his thumb and clamps down, testing it.

Satisfied, he nods to Joe.

Joe then signals to the announcer up on a perch that Billy's ready to go.

A moment later, a horn blares and the chute swings open, releasing Wild Child like an explosion into the ring with Billy aboard, riding shotgun.

Wild Child instantly begins to kick, flailing his hind legs in a jaw-dropping display of terrifying strength, whip-lashing Billy like a rag doll as he hangs on for dear life – each furious second like a brain-rattling century – only to suddenly feel himself jettisoned ass-over-tea-kettle into the air, to land headfirst with a head-crunching thud into the turf, inducing a communal groan from the gallery.

As Ray and Kooch leap to their feet, instinctively grimacing, rodeo clowns rush out to divert Wild Child's angry attentions long enough for a pair of rescue cowboys to hurry over to Billy, lift him up, throw his arms over their shoulders and tote him to safety, dragging his toes in the dirt.

In the stands, folks shake their heads, feeling Billy's pain as the ring announcer expresses their wincing sentiments:

Whooie boy, is that ever gonna smart tomorrow? Better luck there next time, Billy.

2

Later, as Ray swats flies from his neck, Billy walks out from the makeshift First Aid tent with his arm in a sling and wearing a pair of those stupid-looking, disposable dark glasses that always follow a concussion exam.

Ray looks up, biting his tongue. But Billy knows that look:

Let's just go.

As they walk through what looks like a used, pick-up truck lot, Ray ventures:

So what'd the nurse say?

She said I should have my head examined.

Ray can't resist:

Now that's what I've always said.

As they arrive at Ray's old Ford pick-up, Billy takes a last look back at the colorful Fair Grounds:

Sally said she'd come. Ya see her?

Ray shakes his head, not exactly a fan of Sally.

Let's just go.

Climbing into Ray's truck, Billy muses:

Why do I always draw the loco ones?

Ray looks over, still on the subject of Sally:

Women?

Billy scowls:

Bulls!

Ray shrugs, well aware of Billy's history when it comes to romance:

If I were you, Billy, I'd be more concerned about them women of yours.

As they speed along, Ray glances over to see Billy's lips moving, reflecting on something, talking it through to himself. So Ray finally inquires:

You were sayin'?

Ya can't really blame a bull for buckin', Ray. He's just tryin' ta claim his dignity best he can, even if the world's got him all penned in.

Ray ponders, appreciating Billy's sentiments until Billy adds:

And it ain't "women". It's one woman. Sally.

Ray privately shakes his head as Billy makes his case:

All I really gotta do is awaken the romance buried deep in her soul.

Ray's about to be sick:

Oh it's buried deep all right. Know why? Cause it's dead.

Billy looks over at Ray, taking issue:

Know what your trouble is, Ray? Ya just don't understand about romance.

Ray shrugs, hoping to avoid the topic:

Yup. There's my trouble.

A speeding car suddenly smashes into them, tumbling their truck end over end in a metal-shredding, glass-shattering crash, leaving only a blaring horn to call for help.

Next thing Billy hears is the periodic beep of an EKG machine. As he slowly cracks open his eyes, he discovers his neck in a brace and his legs in traction.

Coming to, he manages to tilt his head just enough to find Ray, dozing in a chair by his bed:

Ray?...Ray?

Ray startles to life:

Whoa! ...How ya doin'?

What happened?

Car hit us. Couple of runaways from Foster care. Not a scratch on 'em.

Billy looks back at his immobilized legs:

What's with my legs?

Just then, Chelsea, an East Indian nurse in her late twenties, enters to adjust his pillows:

Good morning. I'm Chelsea.

Billy eyes her, not sure what to do:

You a doctor?

A nurse. Dr. Lopez will be right in. Can I get you anything?

Billy glances at Ray:

Can ya get me yesterday back?

Minutes later, Dr. Lopez, in his fifties with jet black hair, show Billy and Ray an x-ray of Billy's leg injuries:

With compound fractures here, here and...here.

Ray hides a wince as Billy asks:

So how long till I'm up and kickin', Doc?

With the right care and rehabilitation, typically 15 to 18 weeks.

As Billy turns pale, Dr. Lopez realizes this isn't the positive news he thought it would be:

I'll be tomorrow to check on you. All right?

Lopez smiles and heads off on his rounds as Billy, horrified, turns to Ray:

15 to 18 weeks?

Ray tries not to look worried:

Just have ta figure it out as we go along.

Billy storms over, trying to come to terms with what this could mean, and then says:

Ya call my brother?

Took some doin' to hunt him down. Turns out he's in Arroyo.

Billy cocks his head, confused:

Arroyo?

The yo-yo in Arroyo.

Billy scowls:

He's not a yo-yo, Ray. He's got a nice job, a good wife, and I'll bet ya he's even got a nice, new house, too.

Ray lets it go as Chelsea comes back in with a file:

I was just going over your paperwork and you listed the "Silver C Ranch" as his employer and his residence?

Ray nods:

Got us a couple of trailer-homes up there on the south mesa.

Chelsea checks a box on the form:

So your insurance would be under the Silver C's policy?

Billy's confused:

Insurance?

Billy looks to Ray, who responds:

We're just a couple of hired hands, ma'am.

Chelsea can't help betray a look of worry as she reconsiders how to handle Billy's paperwork. Ray notes her look and asks:

So what's a hospital charge for somethin' like this, roughly speakin'?

Chelsea doesn't want to scare them:

I really couldn't...

But when she sees both of them looking at her, needing the truth, she obliges:

Very roughly speaking? Emergency surgery on both legs, intensive care...could be around 25 to 30 grand.

She sees Billy and Ray's faces go blank.

But that's not counting the physical therapy he's going to need.

Billy balks:

Physical therapy?

To help you walk again.

Billy sobers, only now starting to understand what this means.

She can see his devastated look, so she hastens to add:

But, based on your income, you probably won't have to pay all of it out of pocket. Or even most of it.

Ray nods, trying to look grateful:

Appreciate ya letting us know where we stand.

Billy hears the word "stand" and glares up at Ray.

Chelsea, meanwhile, begs her retreat:

I'll check back on you later.

As she moves off, Billy looks heavenward, wondering what he ever did to deserve this:

Now what am I supposed ta do?
We'll figure it out.
But what if we don't? I got bills ta pay, Ray. Hell, how'm I gonna make my trailer payments flat on my back?!

Ray, feeling himself succumbing to Billy's mood, tries to buck them both up:
Now come on. We'll find way. Just gonna have ta take this one step at a time is all.

Hearing the word "step", Billy glares up at Ray again.
Ray winces:
Oh you know what I mean!

Days later, as Ray walks up to the nurse's station he finds Billy in a wheelchair with his legs in white plaster casts from his knees to his toes, signing a Hospital release form, which he then hands back to Chelsea:
The Business Affairs office will be in touch.
Billy smiles darkly:
I expect they will.
Chelsea smiles, concerned about Billy and Ray:
Can I call you a wheelchair-ready cab?
Ray tips his hat.
No, thanks. We're good.

Minutes later, Billy's windblown. Perched atop the wheelchair, roped to Ray's loaner truck's flatbed as Ray speeds them back to the Silver C Ranch.

Billy looks out at the rolling hills and prairie grasses, taking in the landscape of his life, his world, feeling helpless.

A half hour more, and they turn onto a dirt road, passing under an iron trellis with scripted metal letters that read: "Silver C Ranch".

The dirt road winds up into the hills, bringing with it a bumpier ride. Billy winces with every new jolt and dip as Ray navigates them to the top of a dusty mesa where two trailers await them, browned by the ranch and weathered by the sun, connected up to a water line with garden hoses, and an electrical line tied to a small generator.

Ray climbs out and unties Billy's wheelchair. Moments later, he maneuvers Billy's wheelchair into the narrow door of the trailer to find an even more cramped quarters, messy as Billy left it.

As Ray continues to struggle to maneuver the wheelchair, Billy finally waves him off, irked, and tries to maneuver the chair in the confined space for himself, quickly becoming so frustrated that he slams his fists into its armrests:

Goddamn gopher hole of a home!

Ray looks around, knowing it's not going to get any easier, but still tries to find a silver lining:

On the bright side --

Billy balks:

Ain't no "bright side"!

Ray persists:

Mr. C said he'd chip-in for someone ta help ya out.

Help me out how?

Make your food. Clean up after ya. Heck, maybe even do some of that therapy Chelsea said ya gonna need.

Billy's eyes storm:

Yeah, that's what I need: some perfect stranger crowdin' around in here with me!

Ray shrugs:

Well, it ain't like I'm gonna be able to help ya out much, least during sun-up hours.

Billy shakes his head accusingly:

So what are ya gonna do, just leave me here ta rot like road-kill?

Ray's well acquainted with Billy's dramatic side, but this is testing even his patience:

No, cause if ya were road kill, I'd have left ya out there on the road. Not ta mention with you laid up, I got double the chores, Billy, which still need ta get done or Mr. C's gonna find himself some other boys ta get them done, if ya see what I mean.

Billy reconsiders:

Mr. C's a goddamn cheap bastard.

Most rich folks are. So it's time ta deal with things the way they are and stop worryin' 'bout why they ain't the way we want 'em.

Billy's cell phone rings. Ray answers it for him:

Hello? -- No, it's Ray.

He covers the phone to explain:

It's Chelsea, from the Hospital. -- Yeah? No kiddin'. ...Sounds good.

Billy senses Ray's making plans:

What sounds good?

Ray finishes the call:

Will do. And thanks much!

Ray hangs up and looks over, encouraged:

Chelsea's got a friend.

So?

A physical therapist friend.

So?

So maybe she can help.

Billy sneers dismissively. Ray shakes his head:

Now why ya wanna be like that?

Cause I'm dealin' with the way things are, Ray, like ya said, and the fact is I can't afford help, much less my bank loan on this gopher-hole-of-a-trailer, much less my Hospital bill! Hell, I'd have to work over a couple of months just ta afford that pain medication that doc proscribed!

Ray allows him to settle and then replies:

Can I finish? The reason Chelsea suggested her is that she don't have her license yet, so . . .

Billy explodes:

Don't have her license?!

Ta practice here in the States.

Well she sure-as-hell ain't gonna "practice" on me, Ray!

Ray looks heavenward, hoping for some kind of divine intervention, and then turns back to Billy:

Point is, she's got an Indian license ta practice physical therapy, but not an American license, which is why she comes here in the first place.

Billy's still suspicious:

Come here from where?

Ray shakes his head, trying not to lose his patience:

India. Okay?

Ya mean she's come from a Reservation?

Not that kind of. . . She's an Indian from India, which is somewhere over there on the other side of the world.

Ray looks to Billy, expecting him to ease his mind, but Billy has another problem:

That is your way of sayin' she can't talk English?

Ray takes off his hat, rubs his hair back incredulously, and puts his hat back on.

She can talk English, Billy. Probably better than the both of us put together, all right? . . .Point is, ya need someone, and since doesn't have license she needs ta work for cash, on account her student visa somethinoruther.

Billy snarls:

What cash?!

Whatever cash Mr. C's willin' ta chip in, okay?

Billy deduces what the situation is, and sums it up with:

She's here illegal, ain't she? I don't got enough troubles, but now ya want me ta let some unlicensed, illegal alien from halfwat 'round the world crowd in here with me?

Ray eyes him, at his rope's end:

Yes. In fact, given your situation, ya'd be damn fortunate ta have her.

Would I? Well too bad cause the answer's "no"!

Billy waits, expecting a fight, but Ray resigns, disgusted, just tips his hat and climbs out of the trailer without another word:
Where ya think you're goin'?
Ray calls back:
Home!
Billy hears Ray go into his neighboring trailer, so he yells:
What, ya just gonna leave me like this?
Ray calls back:
Good luck, Billy, seein' as ya don't need no one's help.
Billy sits there a few moments, fuming, incredulous:
...Are ya kiddin' me?
But only silence answers.
Billy looks around, marooned.
He then rallies, ready to show the world he doesn't need any help. Yet when he tries to undress himself, he finds he can't. So he tries to navigate his wheelchair nearer to his bed, but he can't:
Sonofabitch. -- Ray?
Silence.
I know ya can hear me, goddamnit!
Still no reply.
Billy grits his teeth, helpless. Finally:
All right, ya made your damn point!
Ray climbs back into view, having been standing just outside the door the whole time, and hands Billy's cell phone to Billy, already connecting a call:
Think Chelsea might wanna hear it from you.
Billy takes the phone, grumbling:
...Shiiit.

As a beautiful new morning gilds over the Silver C Ranch, Billy and Ray look on as a late model Toyota Corolla bumps its way up their service road, stirring up the dust, angling for their mesa. Ray smiles:
Trailin' clouds of glory.
Billy shoots a testy look up at Ray from his wheelchair as the Toyota struggles a bit to make it onto the mesa, where it finally pulls up to park. Out climbs Chelsea:
Hi.
Then the passenger-side door opens, and Mira, also in her thirties, climbs out, lovely as the morning with her black hair, mocha skin and dark, straight-shooter eyes. She exudes a certain self-possession that belies her emotional vulnerability.
Chelsea steps around the Camry to present her:
This is my friend, Mira.

As Mira moves towards them, her steady gaze unsettles Billy, but not Ray, who extends his hand to shake. As they do:

Ma'am. -- This here's Billy.

Mira then extends her hand to Billy, and they shake:

Hello.

Bill nods stiffly:

Ma'am.

Chelsea meanwhile glances around:

Wow. What a view!

Ray smiles:

Couple hundred acres worth. 'Big house is over yonder. And the stables are right over.

Mira takes note:

Stables?

Ray's glad to brag:

If ya like horses, ya come to the right place. Ain't that right, Billy?

Billy shrugs, tight-lipped.

So Ray, realizing he'll need to play the master of ceremonies, opens Billy's trailer door:

So how about we go inside for a chat?

Ray allows the women to enter first, and then out of their view and earshot, confronts Billy:

Would ya relax?

Billy growls back:

You relax!

Ray's about to give him what for, but bites his tongue and focuses on getting Billy's wheelchair into the trailer, and is pleasantly surprised to find Mira and Chelsea immediately pitch in to help.

For Billy, though, their help only makes him feel that much more helpless and humiliated.

As they all squeeze into Billy's little "living room", trying to be polite at close quarters, Ray tries to ease Billy's concerns with some small talk:

So how ya'll know each other?

Chelsea volunteers:

We grew up together in Goa.

She can see neither Billy nor Ray has a clue where that is:

That's in India.

Ray smiles over at Billy:

Never figured we'd get any visitors from India up here, did we?

Billy ekes out another halting shrug, forcing Ray to continue as if he was Billy's personal emissary:

So, Mira, I assume Chelsea filled ya in on Billy's situation?

Multiple stress fractures to the upper right fibula and left tibia.

She turns to Billy, indicating she would like to have a close look at his legs:

May I?

Before Billy can say no, Mira's already kneeling before him to inspect his casts:

With these kinds of injuries, it's best to start therapy right away.

Billy reacts:

Now just hold on a minute. 'Fore we all go ridin' off inta the sunset together, think she should know Mr. C's gonna be payin' her, which means it's gonna be less than a little.

Mira looks to Chelsea, whose expression suggests she may not have fully briefed Mira on the facts of this job, forcing Mira to inquire:

How little, exactly?

Ray jots down Mira's pay on a pad, and hands it to her.

As Mira eyes the sum, sobering, Billy shoots an "I told ya so" look to Ray.

Ray, worried they'll lose Mira, tries to sweeten the deal:

What if we was ta throw in a year of free ridin' lessons for the both of ya? Ya could come anytime, ride as much as ya like --

Chelsea's eyes brighten:

Really?

Mira looks to Chelsea, and Chelsea catches herself:

I mean, depending of course on...

Ray and Chelsea look to Mira, hanging on her decision as Billy looks out the window as if he's expecting the deal to go south.

Mira, caught between her need to make some cash, and a client who doesn't seem to want her, finally utters:

Thanks, but...no.

Ray, trying to hide his growing desperation to secure her, takes another shot:

Ya sure, 'cause Billy could teach ya ta ride.

I'm sure he could, but...no thanks.

As Ray deflates, Chelsea takes up the cause:

Her pay would all be in cash, right?

On the barrel, and up front.

As Chelsea looks to Mira, hoping she'll change her mind, Billy looks to Ray as if he'd known this would happen from the get-go.

Minutes later, as Chelsea drives Mira back down the service road, Mira stares out the window, wearing the look of someone who's questioning their every life decision.

Chelsea glances her way, concerned:
Didn't mean to put you on the spot.
You didn't. And God knows I need to make some money.
Chelsea can't help herself:
And it is in cash.
Mira considers it and then looks out again at the golden hills, feeling doomed:
Why did I even come here in the first place?
Chelsea's confused:
Here? Now?
Mira looks back at her, equally confused:
No. I mean to America. What was I thinking?
Chelsea shrugs:
You were thinking what most people in the world think: that you could make a better life for yourself.
Mira marvels at her misplaced confidence:
Or was it all just some pathetic need to prove myself...Only thing I proved is what a complete and utter fool I can be.
Chelsea sobers:
If you go home on that expired Visa, you won't ever be able to come back. You realize that, don't you?
Mira looks over, suddenly revealing her steel:
Go home? And give them all the satisfaction of saying "We told you so"? No way! I may be a fool, but I am not going to be their fool.
She suddenly deflates again:
. ...Because I'm my own damn fool.
Chelsea shrugs:
Who could use some cash!
Mira looks back over at Chelsea, who shrugs:
Even damn fools need to eat.

Meanwhile, back on the mesa, Ray's sitting in his own trailer, eyeing Billy's trailer, worried. He then looks down at the piece of paper with the cash offer they made to Mira.

On impulse, he suddenly galvanizes with a better offer, one Mira would never expect, but just might accept, and picks up his phone to call her...

~*~

As the first rays of a new dawn break over foaming waves and white-sand beaches of Goa, India, a small fleet of brightly painted fishing boats make their way back from the morning's catch.

A little way up from the beach, a modest room with shuttered windows indicates its occupants are still asleep.

Manhar and Pita, Mira's parents married for some 37 years, are lying in bed, still dozing as their beside phone rings. Manhar gropes for it:

...Hello?

It's me, papa.

Mira? Is something wrong?

No. Everything's fine. I'm sorry to call so early, but I was just wondering how mama was doing?

Pita stirs, so Manhar slides from bed and steps out into the hallway:

Her blood pressure's high and her memory's getting worse. So when are you coming home?

Mira considers what to say, but then lies:

Soon as I pass my Boards, Papa.

But you already passed your Boards here, in India.

Mira endures:

We've been through this, dad.

No, Mira, we're going though this, as we speak, and you're going to regret it.

~*~

Billy again awakens to the faint sounds of the hooves rustling the dirt and dried grass as they make their way out to pasture.

He smiles, and for a moment imagines he's out there with them, only to have his reverie shattered as he drifts back to gaze back down at his leg casts.

Having made a heroic effort to get himself squeezed into the trailer's tiny bathroom, he then eyes what it's going to take him to extricate himself, not to mention pull his underpants back on.

As he eyes the daunting task ahead of him, he hears a car pulling up outside, and it dawns on him it must be Mira, and he blanches, terrified at her finding him like this.

As he struggles up, trying to extricate himself from the bathroom, pull up his britches, get the toilet flushed and get himself back into the wheelchair, he hears her opening his trailer door.

Mira enters maneuvering a massage table as best she can to hear a strange series of thumps, bangs and suppressed yelps coming from the bathroom:

Billy? It's Mira...You okay?

Fine!

As the unsettling sounds continue, she approaches the bathroom and peeks in to find Billy caught betwixt and between the toilet and wheelchair, mooning her:

Do ya mind?

But Mira seems matter-of-fact about it all:

Why would I mind?

Billy's about to explain, but then realizes she's already assisting him, despite his best efforts to avoid her help.

Making matters worse, she routinely pulls up his underpants, and then his pants to his utter shock and alarm. She then sits him back into his wheelchair without batting an eye:

There. Better?

Before he can give her a hundred reasons why this is not better, given that she's seen his privates, she's already unfolding her massage table, struggling to set it up in the small kitchen area of the trailer:

Time for your exercises.

He eyes the table, still reeling:

On that rickety thing?

I'll need you on your back.

Billy takes a moment to consider all the ways in which the universe apparently intends to humiliate him today.

On my back?

I'll help you.

Whoa, I first wanna know what ya think you're gonna do ta me?

We'll begin with some breathing exercises.

Why?

Because we need to get your blood moving.

She pats the table, indicating she needs him on it.

Ya sure ya know what you're doin'?

Very sure.

Minutes later, he finds himself atop the massage table, looking up at her warily as she instructs him to:

Breathe in…

Mira inhales, demonstrating, but then sees his dubious look:

This isn't for me. I'm still wondering if it's for anyone.

Mira gives him knows-better look and repeats:

So, deep breath in.

Billy half-heartedly follows her lead.

Hold it in…and exhale.

They exhale together.

And again, deep breath in…hold it…and release.

Billy exhales, wondering what the hell good this is doing as Mira persists:

And again, deep breath in…hold it…and let it out.

He exhales, his skepticism turning sarcastic:

14

Ya cured me, Doc.

But Mira moves on, unperturbed:

Now this time, when you hold your breath in, I want you to try to gently flex your calves.

He looks at her as if she's lost her ever-lovin'-mind. She replies simply:

By pointing your toes.

Ya serious? Cause if I could dance, I wouldn't exactly need your help, now would I?

Mira dismisses his complaint and proceeds:

And deep breath in –

Billy begrudgingly obeys.

Hold it...and flex!

Billy tries to ever-so-gently flex, only to trigger a searing surge of pain up his legs:

Jesus!

She braces him, not surprised as the pain echoes through him, slow to fade:

Lord almighty!

He looks up at her, incredulously:

What the hell, lady!

And deep breath in...

No way. I ain't tryin' that again!

It will help with pain. Now take in a deep breath.

Just about at the end of his rope, he draws in another breath.

Okay, hold it...and flex.

Billy, holding his breath, shakes his head "no".

She tries to encourage him:

Come on, you can do it.

But he just shakes his head:

This is what will get your blood moving to where it can do some good.

Bill belches out the air, shaking his head:

What part of "no" don't ya get?

Ray, trotting alongside the herd, looks up to see the Toyota's dust-trail as Mira drives back down the service road, leaving the mesa.

He checks his watch, concerned:

Already done for the day?

Ray reins his ride around and trots off towards Billy's trailer, as Kooch takes over the watch of the herd.

Ray finds Billy on his bed, staring at the ceiling. Before Ray can make heads or tails, Billy's ready with a demand:

Ray, I gonna need ya ta call Chelsea and tell her "thanks, but no thanks."
Ray's confused:
What are ya talkin' about?
I'm talkin' bout the fact that that friend of Chelsea's don't know what the she's doin'!

Billy's phone rings. Billy can't reach it, so Ray answers:
Hello?
Billy waves off the call. So Ray says:
Sorry, but he's gonna have ta call ya back.
As Ray hangs up, Billy wants to know:
Who was it?
Your bank.
Billy scoffs, only too well aware of why they're calling:
My Trailer payment.
He then shouts to the window as if the bank could hear:
If ya want it so bad, why don't ya just come and take it!
But Ray still wants to know:
Now what's wrong with Mira?
She's dangerous, that is what!
Dangerous how?
Billy can't believe he has to explain this:
A few days of her, and I'll be dead.
Ray ponders it before replying:
On the bright side; if ya do die, they can't collect on your debts.
Billy glares up:
Ya think this is funny? Ya think me lyin' here on what could very well be my death bed is a joke?
Ray has had enough:
Ya ain't gonna die, Billy. But as for those of us around ya, all bets are off.
I want ya ta call her and tell her services are no longer required!
Ray shrugs:
Call her yourself.
Ray heads out, shaking his head as Billy glares after him, livid.
Ya just gonna leave me here?
Next time, don't tell her ta leave. Then ya won't get left!

Outside, Ray, grumbling, mounts his mare and trots off back to the herd, relieved to be back in the fresh air and space…which also makes him glance back at Billy's trailer, knowing Billy would give anything to be back on a horse, trotting out to the herd.

That evening, Billy and Ray are sitting in Billy's dirt patio patch, watching a scratchy black and white TV as Billy broods.

As the first rays of sunlight gleam over the rolling hills, Billy wakes up with a start, eyes the alarm clock, and, good to his former routine, tries to roll out of bed as if his legs were fine, only to feel an explosion of pain.

He yelps, riding it out, and then struggles into his wheelchair, hearing the faint stirrings of hooves, and Ray and Kooch's faint whistles as they guide the herd out to pasture.

Billy grimaces, crushed, and tires to maneuver the wheel to where he can get a view. But he keep banging into things, spiking his agitation, which quickly turns into rage.

He starts grabbing at anything in arms' reach, including three rodeo-riding trophies and heaves them at the prefab walls of his trailer, smashing them into pieces.

He then rips and tears off the cheap, vinyl sliding door of the bedroom and tries to throw it. But it just ends up in a heap on the kitchen floor.

He's sweating now, livid, looking for anything else he can destroy as the familiar sound of the Toyota pulling up seizes his attention.

Realizing he's barely covered, he starts looking around for something with which to cover himself as Mira climbs into the trailer:

Billy? It's me, Mira.

Billy manages to partly cover himself with a dishtowel as Mira bangs in with her massage table. She nods to him pleasantly, sees the ripped off vinyl door, and then notices the smashed trophies and the dishtowel.

By way of explanation, Billy offers:

I was...tryin' ta create some space in here.

Mira considers it matter-of-factly and then says wryly:

I was wondering when you were finally going to get around to that.

He eyes her, simultaneously suspicious, amazed and flabbergasted that she doesn't seem to be bothered by the fact that he clearly just threw a tantrum. In fact, she looks cheerful:

Anyway, it's time for your exercises.

He grumbles:

I don't feel like exercisin' today.

Mira shrugs:

Only blonde girls named "Tawny" feel like exercising every day. But you do want to walk again as soon as possible, right?

She hands him a clean, white towel, offering far better coverage.

Shall we begin?

A minute later, Mira leads Billy through his exercises again as he lies on her massage table:

And deep breath in, hold it, and exhale. And again, deep breath in, hold it...and release.

Billy snarls:
My legs are broke. Not my lungs.
Mira counters:
Which is why you're going to flex your leg muscles again, thereby increasing your blood flow to the injured areas so that you can speed your recovery – or would you like me to go over that again for you??
He gives her another sneer, apparently trying to create a dust-up:
Ya just don't understand, do ya?
Understand what?
What this is like! Ya ever get both your legs broke?
She shrugs, conceding she hasn't, and Billy immediately seizes on that fact:
So ya really don't have any idea what it's like ta go from taken care of your business, ta lyin' helpless on some rickety table while some stranger telling ya what ta do!
Mira stops to consider it and then nods in agreement:
I'll bet it sucks.
He's about to take issue, but then realizes she's agreeing with him:
What?
She shrugs again:
You're right. I don't know what it's like to have both legs broken. But I do know what it feels like to be helpless.
Billy eyes her, wondering what she's referring to as she continues:
And what I also know is how to get you back on your feet sooner than later. So what's it going to be?
Billy eyes her, trying to get a fix on this unpredictable gal:
Do I gotta choice?
How about we get back to your exercises? …And deep breath in…

Across the mesa, a sudden, painful cry can be heard from Billy's trailer, alarming some gophers as it scatters some crows.

Mira helps Billy lie back onto his bed as he stares at the ceiling, feeling like a torture victim as she gently pulls a sheet over him:
OK, let's talk nutrition, shall we?
Billy, spent, can't even look at her:
No need. I'll be dead by the weekend.
Mira continues:
The point is, if you aren't eating right . . .
Can we talk about this another time, please?
Mira catches herself:
…Okay. Do you have any other questions or concerns before I go?

Billy thinks and then reveals something that's been bugging him, and gestures at the painted mark in the center of her eyebrows:

What's the dot for?

"Dot"?

Between your eyes.

It dawns on her:

I'm Hindu.

Billy chews, not sure if he's buying that explanation. She can see he's skeptical:

What?

If it's cause you're Hindu, then shouldn't it be like an "H"?

Mira eyes him a beat, not sure if he's kidding, but then realizes he's not:

The dot represents the third eye.

He's not sure if she's kidding, but soon realizes she's not:

What third eye?

The third eye of spiritual awareness.

—He is pondering it.

It's not a physical eye.

So it's like a religious thing?

Yes.

Billy ponders this for a moment before remarking:

I know plenty of religious folks who go ta services regular, only I happen ta know for a fact they ain't got no interest in spiritual awareness.

A smile, knowing smile, breaks across her lips:

So do I.

They eye each other. Then he continues:

But boy, do they like ta talk!

Yes they do.

They look at each other again and then Mira comes back around to her main concern:

So what do you usually have for breakfast?

Whatever I can find.

A moment later, she searches Billy's cupboards, finding a can of old Crisco oil, a dead flashlight, and a dusty box of "Trail Muffin Mix".

She calls to him:

When was the last time you went shopping?

Spring.

His phone rings. Mira takes it in to Billy, hands it to him and then moves back into the kitchen to see what else she can find. As she looks around, she hears:

Now just hold on. I've always paid my way. So's even if I don't have the kinda money wheres I can... Collection Agency? How's them takin' my trailer gonna get ya'll paid? ...Well do what ya gotta do!

Mira waits as the trailer goes quiet. She then considers what to do, and a moment later goes back into his bedroom to ask:

You hungry?

Billy, too lost in his upset, dismisses her:

No. And that'll be all for today.

She comes out of the kitchen, folds up her massage table, and, thinking it best to just leave, leaves.

That night, Billy and Ray are sitting in Billy's dirt "patio" again, watching "Jeopardy". It seems like a window into an alien world from here up on their Mesa as Billy looks over to ask:

Ya call Sally like I asked ya?

Thought ya didn't want her ta know.

Why wouldn't I want her ta know?

Cause she stood ya up at the rodeo.

Billy shakes his head, incredulous:

I just might marry that girl, ya know.

Ray shrugs:

If ya run outa reasons ta live, I'd say that'd be just the thing ta do.

Billy storms:

If you know so goddamn much about romance, Ray, where's your woman, huh? Where's your lovin' wife?

Ray reflects:

She's out there.

So's the damn wind, Ray!

Ray smiles to himself:

Guess that must be why I feel her in every soft breeze.

As Billy looks over at Ray, caught off guard by Ray's poetry, the um of a vehicle wending its way up the Service Road draws their attention.

Ray stands and squints into the evening to see who it is. But Billy is impatient:

Well, who is it?

Looks like yo-yo.

My brother Dodger's here?

Ray nods:

Time for me ta say good-night.

Billy shoots him a look:

Could stay and say hello, ya know.

No thanks. I just ate.

Ray heads into his own Trailer as a shiny Lincoln Town car pulls onto the mesa as the evening's orange glow fades into purples and grays.

Out climbs Dodger, late forties with a paunch, dressed in a business suit and acting as if Billy is his cross-to-bear in life.

Dodger? What are you doing here?

Came as soon as I could, little bro.

As he steps forward to see Billy's casts more clearly:

Would ya look at you?

Billy shrugs bravely:

Hey, it's even more fun than it looks.

They shake hands as Billy inquires:

So how're things in the world of high-finance?

Usual pain in the ass.

Dodger flops into the patio chair just vacated by Ray:

So what's the doctor say?

Says I'm gonna have ta hang up my spurs for a while.

Dodger leans over, conspiratorially:

Play your cards right, ya might be able to hang 'em up for good.

Meanin' what?

Oh you know darn well what I mean!

Billy's lost:

No, I don't.

Dodger balks as if it's obvious:

Your settlement monies.

Settlement monies?

From the insurance, dummy.

Billy's still lost, so Dodger's forced to explain:

Ray said ya was hit by another car. So their insurance has gotta pa for your pain and sufferin'.

Billy shakes his head:

Not this time.

Why the hell not?

It was two runaways. From Foster care.

So?

So they're two runaways from Foster care.

Dodger winces since Billy just doesn't get it:

So sue their Foster care parents! Hell, I know any number of personal injury lawyers who could . . .

No!

No? What are ya, stupid? Do ya realize how much ya could make off this accident?

Billy shakes his head, refusing the idea.

Dodger's jaw drops:

Ya mean ta tell me I drove all the way here just ta invest your windfall for ya, and now you're tellin' me there ain't gonna be any?

Billy eyes him:

That's why ya come all the way here?

To help you, since you obviously need the help. Only you won't take my advice.

I don't tell ya how ta live your life, Dodger.

Dodger shakes his head, amazed:

Cause I already know how...Jesus, Billy. You live in a shit-hole on another man's land. How ya gonna pay your bills sitting here on your ass, huh?

That's sorta where you come in, Dodger.

Me?

Dodger, worried Billy may ask him for money, glares:

Have you lost your shit-shuckin' mind?!

I don't want your damn money, Dodger!

Dodger expresses his curiosity:

So...what do ya want?

That money left ta us from Aunt Grace? The money ya invested for me? What about it? I need it.

Dodger shakes his head disdainfully:

What ya need is ta go after them Foster parents with both guns blazin'!

No, what I need is what she Aunt Grace left me.

Well, that's not possible, Billy.

Why not?

Cause like you said: it's invested. And it'd take a while ta even begin ta de-invest it.

So begin "de-investin' it", Dodger, 'fore I lose what little I got left.

Dodger tries one last time:

Want my advice? The real play here it ta sue those Foster care parents down ta the bone.

Billy shakes his head.

I need ya ta be my brother, and get me what's mine. Not yours. Just mine.

Dodger, growing evasive, flashes a serviceable smile:

Have it your way, Billy. What are families for?

As Dodger moves off to climb back into his Town car, Ray, spying from his dark trailer, watches him leave and then comes out to help Billy back into the trailer:

So?

So he said he would.

But Ray's none-too-convinced as he pulls the wheelchair back into Billy's trailer.

As the sun creeps over the hills, Mira drives onto the Mesa to find Ray standing by Lucky, a brown mare, saddled and ready to ride.

Mira pulls over and parks the Toyota. Then she apprehensively rolls her window down, staying inside the safety of the Toyota:

Hi.

Ray tips his hat:

This here's Lucky, and she'd like ta know when ya might be available ta ride her.

Mira seems to go a little pale:

Some other time, Ray.

Don't ya wanna maybe just give her a whirl right now?

No. Thanks.

Ray notes that Mira seems to be keeping her distance:

So how's the patient?

Mira smiles:

I've seen worse.

Ray winks:

I haven't.

Ray tips his hat, climbs onto Lucky and canters off onto the hills as Mira watches after him. Only then does she climb down from the safety of the Toyota.

Moments later, Mira steps in to find Billy hiding himself under his bed-covers, like a kid refusing to go to school. She approaches gently:

Good morning.

I can't today.

Mira, sensing his mood, considers what to do:

Have you had anything to eat?

Billy shrugs.

I could make you some muffins.

Bill's surprised:

Ya know how ta make muffins?

It's a mix. How hard can it be?

An hour later, Billy, dressed and wheeled up to the kitchenette table, is staring down at what looks to be small, shriveled black prunes.

He then looks up at Mira, who looks positively flustered, and then back down at what had become of the muffins.

Poor little bastards.

Mira shakes her head:

Something is wrong with your oven, you know.

Billy eyes her and then sees a pot on the stove:

That coffee?

She pours him a cup, but not one for herself:

Ya aren't havin' any?

I don't drink coffee.

Why not?

Because I drink tea.

He takes a sip of the coffee, grimacing at its acrid taste.

Can see why.

Mira shakes her head:

I don't really cook American food.

Can understand why.

Mira gets a taut look as she tries to suppress the tension she always feels whenever she doesn't perform perfectly:

Goan food is what I cook. You like spicy food?

Billy worries he might commit himself to something even worse than this meal:

Sometimes.

I could cook you a Goan meal, in which case, I would have to go to the market to pick up a few things.

Billy looks doubtful.

Or I can stay here and we could do your exercises.

Billy weighs his Hobson's choice. Finally takes out his wallet and hands her a twenty.

Just no dog or frog dishes, okay?

Mira eyes him dryly before responding:

There goes dessert.

As she heads out, Billy wheels to the door to watch after her, not so sure if she was joking or not.

A young steer thunders over a hill, followed moments later by Ray, galloping after it in hot pursuit.

As Ray closes in, the steer turns left, then right, before making a break for another hill. But Ray gallops ahead, out-maneuvering it, forcing it to pull up short.

As the steer and Ray, atop Lucky, face off like gunfighters at the OK corral, Ray tips his hat to it:

Mornin'.

The steer snorts, frustrated, as Ray's phone buzzes to life.

Ray scowls, reaches into a saddle bag and pulls it out:

Hello?

It's Billy:

Ya call Sally like I asked?

Ray winces and hangs up to refocus on the steer:

Now where were we?

Billy, eyeing the photo of Sally, finally screws up the courage and dials her number, only to hear her answering machine field his call:

Hey, there. Sally here. Leave a message and I'll get back ta ya in 2 winks.

Billy's about to leave a message, but then thinks better and hangs up. Then he lets out a primal yell.

Mira meanwhile is wheeling her grocery cart down an aisle stocked with products like "Cheez Whiz", which Mira stops to dubiously read the ingredients of as some locals cast quick glances her way, suspicious she's an illegal alien, which makes her feel even more like an alien, especially holding the Cheez Whiz.

She arrives back at the trailer carrying a bag of groceries to find Billy brooding, apparently leery of what she plans to do next.

So she deposits the bags on the kitchenette table and hands him his change as well as the receipt.

He accepts, now feeling a little awkward about it all as Mira unpacks the groceries. As she does, she notes a photo of Sally in a bikini top and tiny, jean cut-offs, posing as if she's mocking a calendar pin-up girl when the truth is she fancies herself one.

That's Sally. My...girlfriend, mostly.

Mira nods neutrally as she puts away the groceries:

Pots and pans?

Billy points to a low cabinet:

Ya gotta boyfriend back there in India?

She retrieves saucepan and rinses it in the sink:

Things are...different in India.

Different how?

Mira considers how to explain, given the photo of Sally:

We think of relationships more in terms of a life friendship.

She fills the saucepan with water and places it on the stove as Billy absorbs that:

Doesn't sound like much fun.

Neither is divorce.

Billy squints:

Who said anythin' about divorce?

Over half the marriages in America end in divorce in the first 2 years.

Billy considers as she measures out 2 cups of rice. Then he remarks:

If it's friendship you're after, ya can't beat a horse. Or a dog.

Mira looks over, thinking he's kidding, but then realizes he's serious, so she curbs her instinct for a blunt reply with:

I'll keep that in mind.

Billy looks back at Sally, grinning out from the photo as if she's more than any man could want, and then back at Mira as if drawing some vague, unconscious and incomplete comparison in his head. Then he says:

So what brings ya ta America?

Just then they hear a truck pulling up outside.

Billy wheels to his door and opens it to See Travis and Clive Reed, two beefy brothers in their fifties climbing from a big, black Ford Laredo, looking like town Sheriffs in their cowboy hats and boots.

Billy braces, adopting a poker face:

Can I help ya?

Travis takes a slip of paper and reads:

Billy Wilks?

Who wants ta know?

They move closer to his screen door.

Name's Travis, and this is my brother, Clive. We're the owners/operators of the Sunset Collections Agency, and we're here representin' Saddleback Bank, the folks that's carryin' the loan on this here trailer

I know who's carryin' my loan.

Well, then it oughta come as no surprise to ya that the bank's decided ta call in your loan.

Meanin'?

It's due in full by Monday, on account of your missed payments.

So who are you guys, couple a bank lawyers?

Naw. We run our very own collectin' agency. And what we just told was a matter of law, so consider yourself duly informed.

Billy smirks:

I see. So you're the buzzards circlin' a fresh kill, is that it?

Make good on your debt by Monday, and our business here is done.

And if I don't?

Clive, the other brother adjusts his hat:

It ain't your trailer till ya pay for it, Mr. Wilks. And you haven't paid for it, if ya see what I mean.

Travis shrugs, as if he would like to find a way to help:

There is another way. You could take out a loan with us to where we'd pay the bank your mortgage, and you could keep a roof over your head.

Billy balks:

But I wouldn't own it anymore, would I? Makin' your little visit here today is nothin' more than a couple of buzzards circlin' a kill.

Their flimflam exposed, the brothers drop the nice act:

You don't want a roof over your head, Mr. Wilks; have it your way.

Billy eyes the storm:

Better than have it yours, fellas. Now get the hell off my mesa.

Travis glances at Clive; they've heard it all before. He takes out a business card which he tucks into Billy's screen door.

Case ya should come ta your senses.

They then move off, climb back into their big black truck and drive away.

Billy watches them go, seething as Mira looks on, starting to get a better sense of his broken world. And although Billy's embarrassed by it all, and doesn't know what to say, she feels somehow closer to him, more connected despite all that seems to separate them.

That afternoon, as sunlight filters into Bert's Hardware, a great old store, with long aisles and high shelves, Ray enters, jangling a door chime.

As he heads off down a long aisle, taking him deep into the store, he stops to check on some metal clippers, and hears someone whispering nearby.

Curious, he peeks through a shelf into the next aisle over to see a floozy blonde with oversize rings sharing an adulterous kiss with none other than Dodger.

As Ray grimaces, more disgusted than offended, Dodger sees Ray and hustles the blonde away.

Moments later, as Ray steps to the cash register toting a roll of bail wire, the cashier, April, an attractive Assistant Manager in her fifties, beams to life when she sees Ray:

Well, aren't you a sight for sore eyes.

How do, April?

Where ya been, Ray?

Oh seems like here, there and back again. And you?

She smiles:

Looked for ya at the Rodeo.

Ray shakes his head at the memory:

Had ta leave a little early.

I saw. So how's Billy doin'?

Dodger and the Blonde slip out of the store, jangling the door chime. Ray looks over, rolls his eyes and then smiles back at April:

Better than his brother.

April grins:

Thought he looked familiar. But I don't remember her.

Depends what ya mean by "married".

April and Ray share a look. April offers compassionately:

Guess some folks have ta learn the hard way.

Ray smiles, appreciating her way:

Guess so.

Billy's wheelchair's still scooted up to his door, but instead of confronting Travis and Clive, now long gone, he's instead staring out at the hills as Mira finishes cooking a late lunch:

It's ready.

Billy turns the wheelchair, full of a thought:

Whadaya call it in India when somethin' happens nobody planned, but somebody gets screwed?

Karma.

Billy takes that in and then wheels up to the table, hungry as he is wary as Mira serves them each a plate of her steaming rice dish and then sits across from him.

He picks up his fork, expecting her to join him. But she closes her eyes in prayer, forcing him to wait.

She then smiles up and begins to eat with her right hand, sans silverware. He stares, drawing her attention.

What?

Nothin'.

Billy scoops up a bite, and samples it. Mira waits as Billy takes his time. Finally:

It's...different.

You don't like it?

Didn't say that.

Mira isn't sure what to believe:

So what are you saying?

Billy tenses:

Can ya give me a minute?

Mira waits as Billy slow-chews another bite, sips some water, and chews some more:

So whadaya call this?

Sheeth Kodi.

He gives her a suspicious look, so she translates:

Curried rice.

What's it got in it?

Mira eyes him blankly and then replies:

Curry and rice.

As he looks down at it, considering whether to have another bite, Mira lists the other ingredients:

And bell peppers, and garlic and chutney and raisins.

He absorbs all that:

So this is what ya'll eat in India?

Seamlessly sliding her tongue into her cheek, she leans in:

Actually, it's all we eat, for breakfast, lunch and dinner.

He arches a concerned brow as she presses her jest:

But do you want to know the really strange part? We hate it.

He eyes her confused, trying to fathom India:

But if ya'll hate it, why would ya...?

She leans in closer as if ready to divulge a humiliating secret:

Because all we ever dream about is muffins. Soft, fluffy American muffins. But try as we might, they always come out looking like 'poor little bastards.'

His lips curl as he realizes she just took him for a ride, sealed by her delayed 'gotcha' grin.

Billy leans back, taking it on the chin:
So just how seriously disturbed are ya?
You have no idea.

Mira gets back to cheerfully eating as he watches her deftly fashion her food with her fingers and then sweep into her mouth with a practiced expertise:
If ya don't mind me sayin' so, my mom told me I should never eat with my hands.

She shrugs:
My mom told me I should.
That a fact.

She stops chewing long enough to deliver a well-timed:
"Yup".

As they eye each other like well-matched competitors coming to terms, the afternoon turns golden, filling the trailer with its caressing, warm light.

That evening, down at a local watering hole, Ray's nursing a beer at the bar, relaxing, only to see Dodger and his Blonde enter the joint and make a beeline for a back table. Ray winces privately, throws down a few bucks for the beer, slides off his bar stool and heads for the door only to hear:
Ray!

Ray reluctantly turns to see Dodger waving him over. Ray, disgusted, obliges for Billy's sake.
Hey there, Ray, how ya doin', buddy?

Ray acknowledges him with a nod.
Dodger.
Want ya to meet Tiffany. Tiffany Parks.

Ray dutifully tips his hat:
Ma'am.
So how are things Ray?
Just fine. Ya'll take care now.

Ray heads on his way as Dodger watches after him, irked.

As Ray heads for his truck, he hears:
Just so we understand each other . . .

Ray slows, turns, when he hears Dodger resuming:

Whatever's goin' on between me and Tiffany is between me and Tiffany. All right?

Rays eyes him a beat before replying:
I ain't interested in your business, Dodger, especially that kinda business.
Ray turns and moves onto his rental truck, climbs in and drives off.

As Billy lies in bed, he hears Ray drive up, park, and then enter the trailer. A moment later, Ray steps into Billy's view:
Hey.
Hey.
Billy waits for Ray. Finally:
Somethin' on your mind, Ray?
Ray nods:
Ya get the feelin' Mira's afraid of horses?
Billy's surprised:
Afraid?
She sure looked spooked 'round Lucky the other day.
Billy shakes his head:
Around Lucky? Ya can't get more kind or patient in this world than Lucky. Ya can't. But Mira looked spooked.
Billy considers:
I'd understand if it was, say, Chestnut.
Ray shakes his head as if they were talking about an ornery family relation:
That Chestnut, she likes ta spook.
Exactly. Ya can see it in her eyes, plain as day. But Lucky? No way, Ray. No way is right.
Having said all there is to say for the moment, they nod good-night and continue to ponder the problem as Ray heads back to his trailer.

Over the next week, Mira makes her visits, coaching Billy through his painful exercises while Ray and Kooch do the chores, brushing down mares, mending wire fences, herding cattle and bailing hay.

One day, Mira drives back down to the Highway, but instead of continuing home, she pulls over and parks. A minute later, Ray pulls up behind her in the truck. She gets out of the Toyota and climbs into his truck, sharing a knowing look as Ray throws the truck into gear, and drives off, heading back into town.

An hour later, Mira and Ray are sitting quietly in the county court office, awaiting their turn.

In short order, Ray drives Mira back to the Toyota, and, after a parting, appreciative nod to Ray, she climbs back into the Toyota and drives back to her apartment as Ray drives back up the service road to the trailers.

More days and weeks pass of their routine, culminating with Billy and Mira having a picnic under a shady tree overlooking the Silver C Ranch. Mira smiles reflectively:

Reminds me a little of where I grew up. Except that all would be ocean.

Billy, still in his wheelchair, gazes out, trying to imagine it.

You should come to Goa. The beaches are so beautiful. And there's nothing like swimming in the ocean.

Billy winces at the thought:

Thanks, but no thanks.

Mira looks up, amazed:

You don't like swimming?

Ain't much call for it round here. Except in a flood. Which is what happened ta me when I was seven.

A flood?

Damn near carried me across the county. Woulda drown me, too, except for my rain coat got caught on a fence post. Rancher who found me said he had to pump the water outa my lungs.

Wow. That must have been awful

Put me off swimmin', that's for sure.

A moment of silence passes. Billy then looks at Mira:

So ya miss it? Home?

She nods:

Think about it all the time.

Later, as Mira drives them back, Billy looks over:

So when ya fixin' ta head back home?

We'll see.

Billy considers, starting to be concerned she could leave:

So ya think maybe it's on account of Karma you're here?

Maybe.

How about me getting my legs broke; is that karma? Cause if everythin' is karma, how'll ya account for just plain ol' accidents?

Mira reflects:

I think everything has a purpose.

Billy gazes out the Toyota's window a moment to take in the view and then says:

Ever see a dog chase his own tail?

Mira looks over, confused as Billy continues:

Ya tellin' me that's got a purpose?

She makes a face, dismissing his question. So taking up the challenge, he reaches into their picnic basket, finds the mustard, and pulls it out.

So if I was ta say, just happen ta spill some of this mustard on ya, would that be karma, or an accident?

She looks over wryly, noting his sly look:

No, that would be a tragic mistake.

He continues to eye her as if he could, at any moment, smear her with mustard, and she meets his look with an equally "don't you dare" twinkle, and he finally relents:

You're right, until I'm outa the wheelchair, it would be a mistake.

With that, he puts the mustard away, prompting her to smile as he then moves onto another topic:

Can I ask ya somethin'?

Sure.

Do ya like horses?

She hesitates but then answers:

Yes.

Billy notes her hesitation and so enquires:

How 'bout surprises? Ya like surprises?

No.

Billy tries to hide his look of concern:

Maybe ya just hadn't had enough good ones ta where ya could like 'em.

I've had all the surprises I want for one life, thanks.

Back on the mesa, as Mira helps Billy climb from Toyota into his wheelchair, Billy whistles and Lucky, tethered, clops out from behind Billy's trailer.

As Mira tenses, Billy tries to make it a nice surprise:

Say hello ta Lucky. A true friend if there ever was one.

He can see Mira wants no part of this, but he nevertheless wheels over to Lucky, pulls out some sugar-cubes and feeds a few as Lucky 'nickers' contentedly.

Billy then holds up a sugar cube for Mira to offer Lucky, but Mira refuses to approach, exposing her dire fear of horses as never before.

Now come on, Mira, Lucky won't bite.

This…'sn't how to do this, Billy.

Do what?

He smiles, trying to keep things light and airy, even as she turns ashen, slipping into a primal panic.

Won't take but a minute.

Mira steels herself, wanting to try, but beginning to tremble uncontrollably as Billy looks on, realizing the depths of her terror.

Holy crap. Are you okay?

Later, as Mira quietly boils water for a cup of tea, Billy is keeping an eye on her, feeling as guilty as he is confused:

Didn't mean ta...

She shakes her head, not wanting to talk about it. But he can't let it go:

Remember, a horse is just as scared of you as you are of it.

She coolly places a tea bag into a cup, still reeling:

Anyway, I thought...

Billy finally realizes there's nothing he can say, and bites his lip as she brings her tea to the table, and sits down to stir it. His phone rings, and he wheels around to answer it:

Hello?

Billy's face instantly storms over as he realizes who it is:

Listen Beavis, or Travis, or whatever the hell your name is: don't ya ever call me again, ya understand? You or your damn brother!

Billy slams down the phone, enraged, as a light rain begins to patter outside.

He wheels on to his screen door and looks over the ranch as a crack of thunder rips across the Texas sky, unleashing a brief downpour.

As he stares out at the rain, he sobers, reminded of his troubles.

So what'd I do ta deserve this karma?

He wheels back around to her, challenging her:

If everythin' is got a purpose, then what's the purpose of me havin' my legs broke, and just when I was tryin' ta get my life started? What other purpose could there be but ta punish me for all the things I done wrong? Only I don't know what I did that was so damn wrong as ta deserve this shit!

Billy's eyes hold hers, insisting on a response, so she puts down her tea cup:

The purpose of karma is to teach. Not to punish.

Teach me what? That pain hurts? That not havin' no money in this world is worse than a mortal sin? Teach? I'll tell ya what this is teachin' me: that ya get kicked and punched in this life for reasons or for no damn reason. And especially when ya got less. So whether ya wanna call it an "accident" or "karma", either way ya get screwed when ya got the least chance ta do anythin' about it!

Mira withdraws into herself as he waits for her to argue.

But the more he waits, feeling increasingly convinced he's right, the more distant she seems to become, until she suddenly picks up her bag and hurries out, moving as if her only recourse is to escape.

He watches after her as she trudges out into the rain and mud to climb into the Toyota.

Yeah, go. Run. Hell, I'd join ya if I was the one who's screwed!

Mira meanwhile climbs into the Toyota, fires up the motor and throws it into gear, causing her tires to spin in the mud, but fail to grip.

Not recognizing what's happening, she presses the gas pedal, spinning her tires all the faster, digging them further into the rain-drenched mesa.

Billy tries to call to her, to tell her to stop it, but not only can't she hear him, she's determined to escape, leading to another ten minutes of rising frustration until she's forced to give up.

She then sits there in the Toyota as the rain continues to fall, shaking her head, wondering what she did to deserve any of this.

Minutes later, Billy is privately pleased that her troubles prove his point, so he looks over at her:

What's a matter, trouble with your "car-ma"?

She eyes him, soaked, in no mood, and then goes about spreading a blanket on his narrow, built-in trailer couch.

Billy, sensing he may have pushed things a little, tries to ease the tension:

Can I get ya anything?

But she just holds up a hand indicating she's okay, and implied to please just leave her be.

At which he, wisely, lets her have her space and wheels away a few feet.

'But it's the thought that counts', he tries to counsel himself to little relief. He finally just heads off to bed.

Later that night as the skies clear, Mira lies awake on the narrow, built-in couch, gazing out the window as the ebbing clouds reveal a young moon rising over the soaked hills as the moist, midnight air fills with the scent of wet scrub brush, manure and wild sage.

As the first beams of sunlight glow across the sky, gilding the few, scattered clouds from yesterday's storm, Billy awakens to the sound of Mira making herself a cup of tea in his kitchen, quietly boiling water as she fetches a spoon from his utensil drawer and a cup from the cabinet, then pours the hot water into her cup with a small hiss of steam, followed by the spoon gently contacting the cup in quiet, little pings.

He lies there, listening spellbound, soothed, feeling the longing for a life he's never known.

A few minutes later, he wheels into his kitchen to see her standing there, and he suddenly feels the need to say:

'Bout last night? I was out of line.

Mira thinks about what he has said, feeling the unexpected intimacy of the moment and their evolving connection, coupled with her fear of feeling connected:

34

Let's just forget it.

But he needs to say more:

Think maybe I'm just...spooked. And I don't know why things in my life are the way they are.

Who does, Billy?

Fair enough. But it's hard when...ya always take care of yourself, and suddenly ya can't. And then ya gotta learn ta let someone else take care of ya.

His words hit Mira like a shot, but he doesn't see it yet.

Kinda a hard ta explain if it's never happened to ya.

Mira smiles darkly to herself.

I understand, Billy. Better than you know.

Billy accepts this it and says:

When the day comes for me ta stand again, are my legs are gonna snap out from under me like a couple of dry twigs?

No.

Promise?

Promise.

Just then they hear a Ford truck pulling up outside. Billy braces, thinking it's the brothers, but then hears Kooch calling:

Billy?

That you, Kooch?

Kooch arrives at the door, already rapping on it:

Sugarloaf's about ta heave-ho!

Billy's eyes blaze to life:

Holy crap! We gotta go!

Mira realizes he means her, too.

Where?

As Kooch hurries to lift Billy onto the back of his flatbed in the dark, Mira looks on confused:

Come on. Hop in.

Where are we going?

You'll see!

Not knowing what else to do, Mira climbs into the back by Billy as Kooch rushes back to the driver's seat, and off they go.

They wind along the bumpy service roads, angling for the stables as the sun rises in the east, awakening the world to an achingly beautiful day.

Arriving at the stables, he parks, jumps out and hurries back to help lift Billy's chair back down to the ground and then goes on ahead of them:

See ya inside.

As Kooch heads into the stables, Mira hesitates, and Billy now senses why:

Ya can stay out here if ya like, but you'll be missin' somethin' really good.

Mira enters the stables warily to see Billy and Kooch looking on as Ray kneels beside Sugarloaf, a brown Mare lying on her side in her stall giving birth.

Maybe it's the nurse in her, but Mira, much to her own surprise, finds her fascination for the amazing blood and beauty of birth more compelling than her fear of the mare. Mira moves closer and closer as Sugarloaf's moment comes ever nearer, gently encouraged by Billy, Ray and Kooch's tender talk:

That-a-girl.

You're doin' great, honey-pie.

Just a little more, girl.

As Sugarloaf's newborn finally slips out – wet, slimy and quivering – Ray deftly helps it climb unsteadily to its hooves as mom snorts, exhausted but proud.

Billy beams at Mira, whose face has been filled with the breathtaking miracle of life.

As Sugarloaf's newborn rests quietly by her mom, Billy glances at Ray and Kooch knowingly, and then turns again to Mira:

So what should we name her?

Mira demurs:

I…wouldn't know.

How 'bout "Mira"?

Ray and Kooch smile up, nodding their approval, and Mira finds herself getting misty-eyed:

Ray smiles:

If that's alright with you?

Mira momentarily forgets how to speak, so she nods, beaming back at the boys, and then Mira and her mom.

Billy smiles, musing:

When I leave this world, it's moments like this I'm gonna miss most.

Ray and Kooch grin. They feel it, too.

Later that morning, back in Billy's trailer, Mira leads Billy through his exercises:

And breathe in, hold it, and...

Billy waits for her "flex" instruction, but instead she unexpectedly stops and looks at him squarely. He arches a brow:

What?

Sit up.

Up, as in up?

She helps him up, repositioning him so that his legs hang down, not quite touching the floor:

Now what?

I want you to lean forward and put as much weight on your feet as you can.

Billy's eyes flare open, and he looks at her with alarm:

But...

They won't break, Billy.

Ya absolutely sure 'bout that?

Absolutely sure.

He stares at her, wanting to believe her, but scared to trust:

What if they don't hold?

They will...Promise.

Billy looks down, eyeing the kitchen floor below as if it was a precipice beyond his reach. But Mira urges him on, taking hold of his arm to support him:

Come on.

Slowly, gingerly, he eases down, sliding off Mira's table until his feet can feel the ground. Only then does he ever-so-cautiously transfer a portion of his weight, ounce by ounce, onto the floor as Mira manures to stand right in front of him, eye to eye, face to face, as the haltingl look of fear and revelation play a tug-of-war over his face.

As she helps him steady himself, now standing for the first time in almost 15 weeks, she grins:

How's that feel?

Weird but...okay, I guess?

Now, all of you.

He again looks at her as if she's lost her mind, but her supreme faith moves the mountains of fear inside him aside:

Come on. You can do it.

He takes a moment and then apprehensively allows all his weight to slide from the table, only to momentarily recoil in terror.

You can do it, Billy.

No I can't.

Oh yes you can. Now come on.

So he tries again, stunned that she's convinced him to try again as he eases his full weight onto his legs.

They stand there, looking at each other, silently acknowledging the milestone with a steady gaze that quickly breaks into a shared grin.

Billy's grin then fades as he is filled with emotion, meeting a moment he felt might never come.

Mira then slowly backs away, allowing him to stand on his own:

I'm standin'. On my own two feet...Sonofabitch, can ya believe it? Hot damn, boy!

That afternoon, as Ray rides back from the hills, he sees Billy sitting in his wheelchair, a good way from the trailers, and it worries him:
Now what the heck's he gotten himself into?
As Ray trots over to Billy, Billy calls to him:
I'll bet you're askin' yourself: what the heck's goin' on?
Ray shakes his head:
No, but as long as you're at it, what's goin' on?
Wanna know what's goin' on? I'll show you what's goin' on!
Billy, using his chair as support, slowly but surely stands up.
Ray shakes his head quietly and then takes off his hat and resets it into place. Finally:
Well it's about goddamn time.
Ray then dismounts, walks over and shakes Billy's hand.
They smile. They then hug, patting each other on the back before allowing the moment to slip.
So where's Mira?
Billy points, and Ray turns to see her walking over. Ray smiles and receives her with a bear hug, making her laugh.
Finally got his lazy ass outa bed, did ya?

As Chelsea arrives home from work, tired, she finds Mira combing her hair, apparently preparing to go out on the town, such as it is:
Hey.
Mira looks up, more cheerful than Chelsea remembers:
Hey. How was your day?
Long. How're things for you?
Mira braces, cautious to admit to good news:
Looking up, a little.
Chelsea's ears perk:
Tell me.
Remembering that thing we talked about?
Ray said yes.
Chelsea explodes with relief:
Oh thank god.
She scoops Mira up into a hug.
That is such amazing news. So when are you going to do it?
This week.
Chelsea marvels:
Incredible. So you glad you took the job, or what? So what 'does Billy think?
He doesn't know. And Ray doesn't want him to know.

Why not?

Ray said it would scare him.

Chelsea finds that odd:

Why would that scare him?

Because Ray thinks Billy might think it was up to him to take care of it, and that could screw things up in another way.

Chelsea is increasingly curious:

What other way?

Mira suddenly looks a little tongue-tied. As she struggles to find the words, Chelsea sees something in Mira she's never seen before:

Wait a minute; do you two…like each other?

No! It's not like that.

Mira tries to look certain – to feel certain – for Chelsea's benefit, not to mention her own:

I mean we of course like each other, but it's not like…

Chelsea waits, gleefully encouraging Mira to dig herself into a hole:

Not like what?

Mira, flustered, puts down her brush and turns to Chelsea as if to clear the air of any misconceptions:

Billy stood up for the first time today, so Ray invited me out with them tomorrow night to celebrate. After we take care of the other thing.

Chelsea smiles:

You're right. Things are looking up.

They can hear a live, foot-tapping honky-tonk band as they pull up to the bar in Ray's truck, and park out front with the other trucks.

Billy, using a cane, enters with Mira and Ray to find a small but crowded joint swinging with two-steppin' tunes, beers and flirty talk as the locals unwind, cowboy style.

Ray winks to Billy and then escorts a surprised Mira out onto the dance floor to show her a few turns as Billy draws in a deep, satisfied breath and glances around, finally feeling as if he's back.

He then spots Sally, sipping a beer in a revealing tank top and tight jeans, elbowed up to the bar with her blonde girlfriend, Kelly, pretending not to notice the ranch hands on either side ogling them like rattlers eyeing distracted mice. That is just the way they like it.

So when one tries to actually hit on Sally, her disdainful rebuff sends him back to his buddies with his humiliated rattle between his legs.

As she turns back to Kelly, she sees Billy and she is shocked. Much to the envy of others, she hops off her bar stool and scurries over to give him a big, squealing embrace meant to frustrate their hapless attentions even more:

Oh my god what happened, babe!

Billy's surprised:
Ya mean ya...didn't hear?
Not a thing, babe.

On the dance floor, Ray's showing Mira the Texas Two-Step:
Step, step...that's it. Nice!
Among the onlookers, April steps out of the bathroom to see Ray and glows to life. Mira sees her eyeing Ray:
I think somebody wants to dance with you.
Mira indicates April.
Ray looks over, sees April. April tries to smile as casually as she can and Mira graciously withdraws so that April can make her approach:
Hey there.
How do, April?
Be doin' a lot better if I was dancin'.
Yes, ma'am.
As Ray spins her away, Mira looks on, pleased and then turns to see Sally chatting up with Billy, remembering Sally from Billy's photo.

Her heart instantly tightens in her chest, and her stomach seems to drop as a sobering rush of jealousy tingles through her surprised body and mind. Reeling, she makes a beeline into the bathroom, seeking refuge.

As two GALS gossip about their boyfriends, touching up their lip-gloss in the bathroom mirrors, Mira heads into a stall to ride out the emotions rampaging through her stunned heart.

Meanwhile, Sally, having worked the Billy moment for all its potential attention-getting value, senses it's time to get back to the attentive rattler-hopefuls back at the bar:
Well, it's just so great ta see ya, Billy.
You, too. Lookin' good, Sal.
You always look good, sugar. But I don't wanna be rude to my friend there, so you call me, and we'll get together real soon.
She sashays back to seat, where Kelly leans in to say:
If ya really wanna score in this bucket of losers, Billy's your boy.
Ah honey, I can score with Billy any time I want.
Then ya might wanna close the deal soon, cause rumor is Billy's about ta score himself a fat insurance check. We're talkin' lotto money, honey.
Sally instantly sobers, already formulating a plan:
Ya don't say...My, my, my.

Ray, having watched all this even as he dances with April, starts looking around for Mira, concerned.
April senses his preoccupation:

Somethin' the matter, Ray?

I'm sorry, April, but would you excuse me for a moment?

She nods cheerfully, trying to hide her disappointment as Ray moves around the joint, looking for Mira.

Mira, still in the stall and feeling increasingly nauseous, throws up into the toilet, suddenly feeling very far from home.

When she finally steps from the stall the primping cowgirls give her a wide birth as she steps up to a sink to wash her hands and mouth.

As she dries up with a paper towel, she eyes herself in the mirror, not to check on her looks, but to come to terms.

The next morning, Billy awakens in bed as usual and checks his watch, expecting to hear Mira's Toyota pulling up any moment.

A half hour later, he finds himself gazing out his trailer windows; then he is stepping out his trailer door to have a look around, wondering where she might be.

Fifteen minutes later he's back inside, eyeing his phone, wondering if he should call.

Five minutes later, he makes the call, and Chelsea picks up:

Hello, Chelsea? It's me. Billy. How ya doin'? Good. Listen, I was expectin' ta see Mira today and...she what?

A prairie rabbit scampers across the highway, darting to safety as Ray races Billy to the airport:

Somethin' about her mother takin' a turn for the worse. ...Why didn't she say somethin'?

What's she supposed ta say?

Billy broods:

I don't know. How about "goodbye"?

Ray, frustrated at Billy, lets him have it:

Maybe she didn't think ya was all that interested.

His words plow into Billy's guts like a combine, churning up his insides.

Don't see what that's got ta do with it?

I know ya don't. Which is why you're gonna have ta find out the hard way.

They pull up to the curb and Billy jumps out to hurry into the terminal, relying on his cane.

Billy rushes around, hobbling as fast as he can through the busy terminal, looking for Mira in the various lines for International flights.

Thinking he sees her, he descends on a woman who turns at the last moment to reveal she isn't, forcing him into an apologetic retreat.

Sorry.

Billy continues his search, riding an emotional roller-coaster until he's about to give up when he hears:

Billy?

He wields around to see Mira, shouldering a carry-on bag, beautiful to him like never before. Feeling his heart swell in his chest, aching, he moves to her:

What are you...?

I'm going home.

Billy glances around, trying to process this:

Now?

She smiles understandingly:

You can stand in my check-in line with me, if you want.

He nods, and escorts her to the line forming to enter the flight gate area:

So how long will ya be gone for?

Mira's face turns thoughtful:

Maybe for a while. A long while.

But what about passin' your Boards here?

Mira shrugs:

Already passed them. In India.

Billy grimaces:

But ya can't just go and not come back, Mira.

That's what my family said when I left India.

But I'm not talking about family. I'm talking about...

Mira waits, but Billy doesn't yet know how to finish that sentence. As he struggles, unsure of himself, feeling a growing desperation and panic rising up inside him, yet frightened of the antidote, all he can do is eye her like a lonely dog.

Sensing his struggle, but also well-acquainted with its limits, she gently leans forward and kisses his cheek as an Airport Security Officer motions her impatiently forward while signaling Billy to stay put:

Goodbye, Billy.

Billy watches after her, crestfallen as she heads on her way, disappearing in the Boarding Gate crowds.

As Ray waits in his truck, watching the planes come and go, Billy arrives to climb back in.

Ray looks over, expecting to hear what happened, but Billy just shakes his head:

Let's just go.

They make the drive back without so much as a word between them, with Ray occasionally glancing over, recognizing the irresolvable pain Billy must be feeling, the pain primed especially for those who do not yet know their own heart.

As the long day gives way to afternoon, they arrive back up on the mesa to see an unfamiliar Ford Escort. It is explained a moment later when Sally, dressed to seduce, Texas-style in a mini skirt, boots, and a low-cut T-shirt, climbs out with a bag of groceries:
Ray's face storms:
What the hell she wants?

Billy, still reeling, but unfortunately for him, still a little curious, climbs out to find Sally blushing, suddenly all peaches and cream:
Hey there, handsome.
Billy moves to her, still a bit dazed.
What're ya doin' here, Sal?
I just felt so sick about all ya been through, and me not knowin' and all, that I wanted ta do somethin' ta cheer ya up.
Ray, meanwhile, makes a disgusted beeline for his trailer. Sally senses he can see right through her, so she momentarily tones down her gushing:
Hey there, Ray.
Ray tosses Billy a look and then steps up into his own trailer, allowing Sally to get back to work:
Look what I got ya:
She pulls out a thawing Sara Lee pound cake, fresh from the frozen food section:
Ta celebrate ya getting' back on your feet and all.
Billy eyes it, feeling, to his surprise, more surreal than seduced:
Appreciate it, Sal.
You better. Had ta go to three different grocery stores and a Piggy-Wiggly 'fore I found it. Can ya beat that?
Billy's not sure how to respond:
Three markets, huh?
So aren't ya gonna ask a girl in?

As Billy looks on, still trying to figure Sally's sudden interest in him, she un-wraps the pound cake as though she was his girlfriend, or wife:
Gotta knife, handsome?
Billy retrieves a knife and hands it to her. She takes it, feigning romantic excitement at his physical proximity:
Guess I shoulda asked for a plate too.

Billy retrieves two plates from the cabinet, coming across the muffin mix. He eyes it a moment, transfixed as Sally waits:

Earth ta Billy Wilks?

He rallies and hands her the plates, but she cuts only one slice of pound cake and serves it to him, to Billy's confusion:

What about you?

If I don't watch my figure, honey, nobody else will.

She performs a runway model's 'turn' for him in the tiny kitchen:

See anythin' ya like, Cowboy?

As the afternoon wears into evening, Ray, concerned, peers out his window, trying to see what's happening in Billy's trailer. But he can't see, so he sinks back into a reclining chair, knowing Billy may well be pissing away his shot at happiness, but also knowing that, just now, interfering might only make that more likely.

Crickets fill the night, singing their songs across a lonely stretch of hills, calling to their hoped-for love, as Billy and Sally, seated at the kitchenette table, finish off a bottle of whiskey over a game of 'Texas hold-'em':

Does the lady-killer man have the ace, or doesn't he?

Gonna cost ya ta find out, ma'am.

Well seein' as I'm runnin' low on chips, guess I got no choice.

Sally makes a sly show of pulling off her tee-shirt, stripping down to her push-me-up bra, and throws it down onto the kitchenette table in place of chips:

Guess I gotta bet what I got – which, fortunately, is a lot.

She smiles, her eyes full of possibilities for the night ahead.

Billy's pulse speeds, but his heart isn't keeping pace, and the conflict between the two suddenly spills out in the flicker of doubt that brushes him across his face, confusing Sally. So she tries to keep the momentum building by challenging him:

What's the matter, honey, can't stand the heat?

Billy smiles, trying to reassert a confident air even though his heart seems to have left town.

Sally can see his mind seems to be wandering, so she again ups the ante:

In fact, it's time ta put it all on the table.

As she starts to undress, pulling off her jeans to reveal a g-string, Billy, suddenly feeling a surge of unease, tries to buy himself a moment by getting up and cutting himself another slice of pound cake and then rinse the dish.

Sally looks on, confused. This is a whole new experience for her, too, and she's momentarily more mystified than offended.

As Billy washes the plate, she tries to draw his attention back to her body:

Maybe ya oughta let that little Mexican girl take care of that, honey.

Billy looks confused:

Mexican girl?

The one I hear ya got workin' for ya!

Billy winces:

Ya mean...Mira?

But Sally's too busy undressing, already down to her bra, g-string and cowgirl boots:

I'm gonna "raise" ya, honey, so ta speak.

Sally grins and pushes her clothes forward as if they were her betting chips, looking as sexy as any pinup girl. But Billy's not reacting to her body, and he's finding that almost as confusing as she is:

Least I hope I'm raisin ya, honey.

She's not Mexican.

Who's not?

Mira.

Who's Mira?

She's Indian physical therapist who's been helpin' me.

Sally's eyes roll:

So she's off the Reservation, for something new. All the more reason she should be doin' the dishes, darlin'.

Billy finally focuses, arriving back from his mental journey to assess his situation, even as he discovers more of his heart.

Sally looks on, frustrated, but still not ready to give up:

Ya feelin' alright there, Billy?

Think ya better go, Sal.

Ta the bedroom?

He looks at her, surprised by her confusion:

No. Home.

Sally nearly falls off his couch, stunned and exasperated:

Home? But ...why?

Sorry, Sal.

Her eyes singe:

Ya tellin' me I came all the way over here just ta give ya a chance to show me what kind of man ya are, and you're sendin' me 'home'?

Billy shrugs, not trying to be flippant or even mean. Just truthful:

Guess ya just...ended up showin' me what kind of woman ya are, Sal.

As she stares at him, incredulous, they hear a car pulling up outside, and Billy looks out to see Dodger climbing from the Lincoln, leaving his blonde behind to wait in the car.

As Dodger walks over, Billy steps out, noting Dodger's date waiting for him back in the Town car:

What's that, Dodger?

Dodger smirks, enduring Billy's quaint morals:

That, my friend, is what ya might call a quick snack on the way home.

As Billy registers his disapproval, Sally, clutching her bra and clothes to her body, leans momentarily into view:

Who is it, Billy?

Dodger smirks, feeling vindicated as Billy is forced to reply:

Be just a minute, Sal.

As she moves out of view again, Dodger shrugs:

Looks like we both got a taste for fast food.

I ain't married, Dodger.

Lucky you, Billy.

They eye each other, neither giving ground until Billy shakes his head:

Ya got my money?

I do. But I'll need one of your blank checks so I can deposit it inta your account.

Billy's confused, so Dodger explains it as though he's a Luddite:

I'll need your bank's routing number, as well as your account number, if I'm gonna transfer your money.

Billy nods, contrite.

Right.

As Billy goes back into the trailer to fetch a check from his check book, Sally looks as if she wants to say something, so Billy finally asks:

What?

She shrugs:

Ain't my business, but why can't he just write ya a check?

You're right, Sal. It ain't none of your business.

Billy rips out a blank check and starts for the door, but then slows and turns, feeling a need to explain things, mostly to himself:

Look, my brother, unlike most the local-yokels round here, is a trained, certified accountant, okay? So I'd say he knows what he's doin', wouldn't you?

Billy steps out and hands Dodger the check. Dodger nods:

Alrighty then.

Dodger starts back to his car, but as he climbs back in he remembers:

By the way, I might be a little out of touch for a while.
Whadaya mean?
What do ya think I mean?
Dodger winks, referring to Tiffany:
Take care, Billy. And don't go burnin' your tongue on any pop tarts.
He indicates Sally with another wink and then climbs into the Sedan and drives away.

As Billy stands there in the dark, watching him go, Sally steps out, trying to salvage whatever she can:
How about we just simmer down, honey, and start over.
Billy turns and smiles quietly:
I just did.
He then steps around her and heads back into his trailer:
Happy trails, Sally.

~*~

Mira's talking to Pita, her mother, who seems at moments to be listening, and at other times seems miles away.
I'm here, mama...Mama?

Later, Mira leans into the family room to find Manhar, her father, watching an American Western on TV:
'Night, Papa.
Good-night, dear.
Mira lingers a moment to watch a TV cowboy chasing down a steer, feeling the sting she had earlier steeled herself against.
Manhar, noting her lingering presence, looks over:
You okay?
She smiles, covering, and moves off.
In her room, she lies down on her floor mat and peers out her window to see the moon rising into view, just as she'd seen it that night from Billy's uncomfortable couch, rising over the Texas hills…

~*~

As Ray gently trains a young mare, walking her around a training corral, Billy walks up, looking the worse for wear.
They trade a worn-in look.
Billy then moves off again, brooding, cresting a hill to suddenly see two men on the mesa, doing something around his trailer.

Billy quickens his pace, wary, suspicious of who they are and what they're doing, only to realize as he moves closer that the men are Travis and Clive, the collection agency boys, and they are hitching Billy's trailer to the back of their black truck. Still too far away to stop them, Billy shouts:

Hey! Whadaya think you're doin?

As Billy hobbles towards them as fast as he can, Travis looks up, sees who it is and flips Billy the birdie but then climbs into the truck with Clive.

Accelerating, they jerk the trailer into forward motion and start towing it off the mesa, destroying Billy's patio as they do:

Stop!

Billy, realizing he can't stop them on foot, reverses pivot and starts hurrying back to the corral:

Goddamnit!

A minute later, Ray turns to see Billy atop Lucky, charging past:

They're haulin' my home away!

Ray galvanizes into action, hurrying to his mount as Billy gallops off, angling across the open hills to cut Travis and Clive off at the pass.

But Billy's struggling, his legs still lacking the strength to control his bouncing body, causing him to flop and slide around the saddle as he strains to keep from falling.

Travis and Clive, with Travis at the wheel, are picking up speed as they tow Billy's trailer down the service road, quickly making their way back to the highway.

They glance at each other, satisfied, but then Travis glances in his rear view mirror to see Billy galloping into view like the Calvary, gaining on them quickly and then adjusting to gallop up alongside Travis's driver side window:

Un-hitch her, damn it!

Travis ignores him. He raises up his window as Billy yells again, livid:

Un-hitch my home, ya piece of shits!

Clive sneers and shouts back:

We warned ya, Wilks!

Travis accelerates onto a straightaway, forcing Billy and Lucky to speed up as Ray crests a hill at full gallop, as yet well behind, but making up ground as Billy once again catches up to Travis's window, about to shout when Billy realizes highway's just ahead, and the trellis isn't wide enough for Billy, Lucky and Travis' truck.

So Billy reins in Lucky just enough to slow her to where she's striding even with the truck's flatbed cargo bay.

Billy then swings his outside leg over so that he's now riding side-saddle – grimacing in pain, scared as hell but drunk with angry adrenaline – and, steadying himself as best he can, leaps from Lucky onto the truck's moving cargo bay much to Travis and Clive's shock and dismay.

Scrambling first to keep from sliding out the back, he son rallies to focus on unhitching his trailer.

Seeing what Billy's attempting in his rear view, Travis starts swerving back and forth, causing Billy to be thrown from side to side, banging his tender legs, forcing Billy to have to focus on just holding on so that he doesn't fall out, losing precious seconds to try to unhitch his trailer.

Travis grins, pleased that his tactic is working, until he realizes Silver C's Trellis entrance gate is coming up fast, forcing Travis to have to straighten and steady the truck to make it through.

So with only seconds to spare, Billy refocuses on unhitching, loosening the safety chains, and then unleashing their safety hooks, until he's suddenly thrown violently to his left as the Truck and trailer pitch, swerving out onto the highway like a runaway train.

Clive blanches, craning incredulously as Travis nearly rolls the truck and trailer as Billy loses his desperate grip and twists out the back, tumbling down out onto the highway hard to roll and bounce away as Travis rights the truck and speeds, home-free.

As Billy lies there on the quiet highway, covered in dirt, bruised and wondering if he's all in one piece, Ray gallops up, dismounts and hurries over, scared:

Billy! ...Billy!

Billy, dazed, slowly opens his eyes to see Ray glaring down at him, half scared to death, half angry as hell:

What the goddamn hell was ya thinking, boy?

Billy eyes him, spent, with no way to explain himself except to say:

I had ta, Ray. I just had ta.

That evening, Billy, reclining on Ray's narrow couch, a wash cloth draped across his forehead, gazes out at the earth-churned spot where his trailer used to rest.

Ray, brooding in his kitchenette, is preparing a meal: beef stew from a can, and fresh, sliced apples.

Billy then takes a swig of some cheap whiskey, a cowboy pain prescription if ever there was one:

It's gone, Ray. All gone.

Ray pours the soup into a saucepan, looking more annoyed than sympathetic as Billy whimpers:

They took my home, Ray.

Ray doesn't respond, so Billy looks over:

My home.

Ray shrugs, in no mood:

Ya mean that little gopher hole; I believe ya called it so?

Oh it was a gopher hole, all right. But it was my gopher hole.

Ray snorts:

Yeah, well, that little stunt of yours almost took your life, which apparently ya was ready ta trade for a gopher hole!

Billy, feeling the whiskey's permission, indulges his feelings:

What "life"? I got no home, no wife. Drownin' in an ocean of debt.

Ray grumbles something. Billy turns:

Ya got something ta say?

Ray balks:

And interrupt your pity party? Far be it from me.

Billy, wanting a fight, spits back:

This ain't no pity-party.

Ray dismisses him:

Everythin' but the balloons, cause Lord know we already got the clown.

Billy, filled with indignation and hurt pride, stares back, incredulously:

Well exuuuse me. Didn't mean ta bend your ear over a little matter like me losin' everythin' I got!

Ray scowls:

Only thing you're in danger of losin' that's worth anythin' is Mira!

Billy stares at him, stunned and then shakes his head, angry that Ray would so readily rub salt in his wounds:

Case ya hadn't noticed, Ray, she's gone. Of her own volition.

Ray gives Billy a matter-of-fact sneer.

And Sally's here, is that it?

Billy's blood boils, despite the whiskey coursing through it.

Ya act as if I somehow sent her away!

Well didn't ya? All but bought the damn airplane ticket.

Billy glares, part stunned, part confused, part guilty as Ray pours the hot stew into two plastic bowls:

Just tell me this: do ya miss her?

Billy rolls his eyes:

What's that got ta do with anythin' now?

Ray persists:

Do. You. Miss. Her?

She's gone, Ray!

So ya don't miss her, is that what you're sayin'?
Their eyes meet, grating now as never before:
No!
Ray shakes his head, disgusted with Billy, which prompts Billy to defend himself:
Why the hell should I? After what she done?
Ray throws down the silverware he'd just collected:
What she done? She done more good for ya than any of them so-called romances of yours ever done!
For the last time, Ray, she's in India!
Then why the hell aren't you, Billy?
A silence grips the trailer as Billy stares at Ray, shaken, livid, in shock...until something finally breaks in Billy, breaks wide open like a dam giving way, or a Texas flood rolling over the plains:
Holy crap, Ray. ...Holy crap.
Ray shakes his head:
Never met a man so intent on avoidin' his own heart. God help me.
I gotta go get her, Ray!
Billy gets up to pace, burning into a determination to go to India and find her as fierce as what he felt when he was to stop Travis and Clive.
I gotta go get her and talk ta her, Ray. Tell her how I feel.
Ray rubs his eyes:
Ya'd be a yo-yo not ta go.
Which means I'm gonna need my money back from Dodger like right away. Only now I don't know where he's at, goddamnit.
Forget Dodger.
I can't. How else am I gonna go?
I'll front ya the money.
Billy's face blanks, too taken off guard at first to even remember to thank him.
Ta go ta India?
Well there sure as hell be no point ta goin' ta Arroyo, now would there?
Billy's eyes burn as he realizes the opportunity Ray's offering him. And a moment later, all he can do is lurch forward to hug him.

The next day, Billy stands at a ticket counter, befuddled:
I need a passport?
An airline employee looks at him as though it is obvious:
Approved by the Indian Consulate.

A few minutes later, Billy climbs back into Ray's truck looking snake-bitten:

What happened?
I can't buy a ticket until I got me a passport and a Visa.
What the hell?
Can ya beat that?
So now what?
Gotta go to the nearest Federal government buildin'.
Ray winces:
Lord!
Billy shakes his head:
It's karma, I tell ya.
What's that?
Billy storms:
In a word? Hell! Now can we just go please?
Ray starts up the truck:
Gonna be one of those days, is it?

~*~

In a square room with marble floors, at a modest but comfortable dining table sit Mira, Manhar and Pita, Elie and Dilip – Mira's sister and her husband – and Alisha, Elie's eleven year old daughter, all chatting with intermingling conversations as they eat their Sheeth Kodi with their hands.

Manhar's voice cuts through the din:
Cammel called.
Manhar looks expectantly at Mira, who nods neutrally as Elie's mischievous nature can't resist commenting:
Little Cammel, all grown up.
Alisha, a straight-shooter in Mira's mold, states what everybody at the table's thinking, namely:
I think Cammel wants to marry Mira now that she's here again.
Manhar shoots a frustrated look at Elie, who obligingly turns to Alisha in a half-hearted show of reproach:
Now Alisha, that's n o way to talk.
Alisha shrugs, not one to mince words:
I think he's in love with Mira.
Alisha! Whatever Cammel may or may not feel is none of your business, do you understand?
Alisha rolls her eyes, not happy to be censored as Manhar tries to avoid the issue altogether:
The reason for his call was in response to my call. All right?
But Mira is shaking her head:
You called him, Papa? Why?

Manhar's blood pressure spikes:

Because my daughter, an Indian-certified physical therapist, needs a job, and Cammel's clinic just so happens to be the very best.

Elie interjects:

You mean his dad's clinic, don't you?

Manhar's excitable nature is getting the best of him:

His dad retired last year, Elie! It's now Cammel's clinic. And why this is any of your business, I'll never know!

Elie shrugs, unimpressed:

Just asking.

Manhar looks heavenward for help:

What is wrong with this family? Why is everybody always in everybody else's business?

Mira can't believe her ears:

Exactly, Papa. So why are you trying to control?

Because I'm your father! And as long as you're my daughter, your business is my business.

Mira looks heavenward in hopes of divine intervention, or at least a divine explanation that can make Manhar understand things from his daughter's point of view.

You don't understand, Papa.

Fine. I don't understand. But I made you an appointment anyway.

Mira winces:

An appointment for what?

A job interview, of course, which he was gracious enough to schedule, based on my long friendship with his father.

Mira and Elie share a knows-better look, which Manhar notes and reacts to:

What?

Elie volunteers:

It wasn't because of your relationship with his dad that Cammel scheduled the interview, Papa.

You two can believe what you like. But an interview is an interview, and I suggest you consider the alternatives before you so easily dismiss my efforts.

Mira feels guilty, and tries to explain:

All I'm saying is couldn't you have asked me first?

Nonsense! It'd be perfect for you.

Mira tries once more to explain:

Isn't that for me to decide?

Manhar snorts:

You're acting like a child.

No, Papa, I'm being treated like one.

Mira, remembering all the reasons why she fled home in the first place, gets up from the table and goes upstairs to her room as everyone left at the table sinks into an uneasy silence which Manhar notes, prompting him to justify his methods:

Once she has the position, she'll thank me.

Pita, Mira's mom, looks over at the stairs after Mira, filled with concern.

~*~

As Ray looks, Billy, elbowed up to a counter, fills out page after page of a form.

Later, standing in front of a white screen, Billy blinks as the bright flash of a passport photo blinds him, burning his vision:

Feels like the damn sun.

Ray, exhausted by this kind of thing, pleads:

Can we go now?

More days pass, driving home more and more memories of Mira as Billy is moving through his daily chores alongside Ray, feeling ever more certain of his coming mission, his heart-compelled gamble, his soul-felt need.

His Passport arrives, and he promptly mails it off to the Indian Consulate down at the Piggy-Wiggly, stopping on his way out to try a call to Dodger from a payphone, only to hear: "The number you have dialed is no longer in service. Please check the number and dial again..."

Billy checks the number, but doesn't dial again.

That evening, as Billy and Ray watch a TV in what's left of Billy's patio area, Billy casts a look at where his trailer used to be. Ray sees Billy looking, and asks:

Ya hear from Yo-Yo?

Billy shakes his head:

Nope.

Ray ponders about the situation and then remarks:

But he was supposed ta transfer your money, right?

Yup.

Ray takes off his hat, smoothes his hair, and replaces his hat:

I take it ya haven't heard from him yet?

Nope.

They share a glance, thinking the same thing:

When you get back, Billy, I think ya best . . .

Yup.

Three weeks later, Billy, squeezed uncomfortably into an airplane seat that won't lean back, awakens confused to the ding of a commercial airplane's public address system, piping in their pilot's accented voice:

Ladies and gentlemen, this is your captain speaking. We'll be arriving at Dabolim International Airport in ten minutes. Please return to your seats. Local time is 11:23am, and ground temperature is 33 degrees.

Billy's face registers alarm. He turns to an Indian businessman seated next to him:

'*He just say '33 degrees'?*

The businessman nods pleasantly:

Monsoon season.

Billy looks at his cotton shirt and jeans, ill-prepared for cold weather:

Don't think I ever been in a Monsoon before.

Then I'm afraid you're in for quite an experience.

As the Businessman buckles up, Billy starts buttoning up his shirt, worried he's about to freeze to death. The Businessman peeks over, confused by Billy's buttoning, but then remembers all white folks are confusing and lets it go.

He limps out of the plane to discover it's incredibly hot and humid. He suddenly sees a world of saris and linen Nehru shirts, feeling as if he's been inadequately dressed:

Thirty three degrees, my ass.

Unbuttoning his collar, he descends the stairs and walks across the tarmac to the terminal, noting the men, some in turbines, and the women and children in vividly-colored cottons.

It's the variety and bold hues that capture his attention first. That, and the heat.

Entering the terminal, he heads for the restrooms, and enters to find a few urinals, but then a series of stalls without any toilets at all – just holes in the floor.

A local catches him looking at the holes:

Must be quite a change for you.

Billy shrugs, assessing them:

Not really. It's more than ya get out there on the open range.

Back in the terminal, Billy canes his way over to a Policeman:

Pardon me, sir, but could ya tell how ta get ta an "Aporo-Noga" from here?

The Policeman winces:

You mean "Arpora-Nagao"?

That, what ya said:

The Policeman considers how to get there:

...You best get to the Majorda station --

Billy goes to make a note with a pen he's brought along, but then, realizing he doesn't have any paper, tries to take the notes on his hand:

That a train station?

Yes. And from there you . . .

Billy holds up his pen hand:

Just one second, how do I get ta that train station?

Policeman shrugs in that Indian way, swiveling mainly the jaw from side to side:

You could take a Taxi. Then take the Northbound to Tivim

Billy stops him again:

Northbound what?

Rail.

And by "rail", you mean "train"?

Policeman's starting to tire of this:

Yes. A train.

Ta where again?

To Tivim.

Billy tries to spell it, but looks to the Policeman for correction:
T.I.V...

"I"... "M". Tivim. And from there you can "rick it" to Arpora. Would you excuse me, please?

Bill asks after him:

"Rick it"?

But the Policeman's already moved off, relieved to be free of Billy as Billy eyes his scant notes up and down his hand and wrist. He then re-shoulders his saddle and one duffel bag and heads out.

On the curb outside the terminal, Billy navigates his way through a sea of travelers, porters and honking cars, all fighting for space along the hectic curbside.

The sheer numbers of people overwhelms him, used as he is to one or two human beings sharing a valley.

As he is starting to be concerned that he's not going to be able to find his way, a plucky 18 year old Indian teenager in a T-shirt and leather flip-flops hurries up, apparently beating out the competition:

Taxi, sir?

Can ya get me ta...

Billy checks his hand;

Majorda Station?

The teen shrugs as if he's been doing it for years:

No problem!

He then commandeers Billy's duffel bag and leads him to a weathered 1983 Ford Taurus:

How long will it take ya ta get there?

The teen smiles:

Let's time it.

Billy, not sure what that means, climbs in as the teen hops in to drive, firing up the Taurus, jerking Billy back into his seat, prompting a passing truck to slam on its brakes to avoid a collision, eliciting a smile from the teen and accelerates them away as Billy looks on, instantly concerned.

The teen speeds the Taurus through the crowded streets, barely missing pedestrians, and then a father, mother and child all riding a motorcycle. He then has to swerve to miss an elderly woman on a bicycle crossing in front and then veers to avoid a sudden cow.

As Billy's eyes pop, thinking this is a lot more dangerous than riding Wild Child, the teen smiles back at him:

First time in India, sir?

The teen skids to avoid a beggar and then turns hard to save a dog pack before accelerating to "thread-the-needle" between a pedestrian and a truck, just missing both as Billy looks on, grimacing:

Holy smokes!

As Billy, now pale, cranes to see if the pedestrians survived, his initial terror starts shifting into a kind of awed respect for the teen's undeniable driving skills. The teen smiles back at him:

Things must be different here from America.

How'd ya know I was an American?

Everybody knows you're an American.

As Billy considers it, not sure if that's exactly a compliment, the teen screeches the Taxi to a stop outside the Majorda station.

Billy's thrown forward in his seat, whipped by the momentum.

Recovering, he sits back, suddenly finding the pace enjoyable:

Well whooooeee, boy!

As the ticket counter is crowded as usual in India, Billy has to struggle to get to the ticket window and then later struggles his way to a window seat on the train, where he sits down across from an Indian family – dad, mom, a girl and a boy – all facing him, all curious.

Billy nods, in a friendly way, as the family nod back:

This the train goes ta Tivim, right?

They smile and nod as the train whistle blows, and Billy lets out a sigh of relief, starting to feel proud of himself.

Billy looks out to take in the view as the train chugs out of the station house to reveal large numbers of men, women and children lining the tracks, as if to bid the train good-bye.

But then they all suddenly rush forward to leap onto the sides of the train.

Billy jumps back alarmed, confused by it all. But then he realizes nobody else seems to be interested or concerned.

So Billy bites his tongue and looks out again to see more and more people swarming down to hop onto the moving train, hitching a ride by expertly knowing just where to grab hold of it, quickly covering the train so that its cars are hidden by the humanity hanging from its sides, or sitting atop the train cars in practiced rows.

And it quickly dawns on Billy that this is just another day on the Northbound out of Majorda.

Later, he gazes out his window to see the lush, Goan countryside flanked by low-lying mountains framing the occasional azure rivers.

Relaxing, he lays his head back, succumbing to the languid lullaby of the train's rhythmic rocking. He dozes like a baby in India's balmy, entrancing arms.

~*~

Ray is standing on a hill, looking out at a stretch of dry bush, apparently making his mind up about something.

An hour later, he walks into a bank branch and looks around for a manager, feeling a little out of place, but very much assured of his decision.

~*~

As Billy comes to, he's greeted by a curious, if concerned, sea of Indian faces, all eyeing him carefully as if he was something like a new zoo attraction.

He sits up to realize he's no longer sitting across from that family from earlier, but a group of teenagers.

He shares introductory nods as they continue to observe him, fascinated.

Would ya'll happen ta know how much longer till we get ta Tivim?
The teens trade bemused looks, worrying Billy.
Why's that funny?
Tivim is where we boarded.
Billy sobers:

Ya mean...this train's already been ta Tivim?

The teens can't help but chuckle as Billy turns pale, suddenly feeling doomed. But the teens aren't mean, and quickly fill him in:

At the next stop, get off, and then catch the next southbound back to Tivim.
Will do. Thanks.

They all share a smile, even if the teens still can't help smirking at his mistake.

But what they told him was the truth, and Billy soon catches the southbound back to Tivim, making sure this time to stay wide awake.

Arriving in Tivim, he climbs off the train and canes his way through the station, amazed at all the people spread out on the floor, using the station as a makeshift hotel.

Realizing he doesn't have any place to go, he too finds a corner to perch his bags as he has so often on the range and then lies back to ride out the night, as accustomed to this as the families around him.

The next morning finds Billy standing at an intersection, looking for some sort of street name or identification. But he can't pick any. So he asks a nearby Rickshaw driver:

Pardon, but could ya tell me where're your street signs?

The driver looks up, confused:

Street signs?
Ya know the signs where they say the name of the street you're on?
Ah, yes. Street signs, of course.

Billy smiles, glad to be understood:

Exactly. So where are they?
Not here, I'm afraid.
No? So where would I find them?

The driver shakes his head:

Not anywhere, I'm afraid.
Why not?
Because there aren't any.

Billy stares at him beaten and then asks in dismay:

No?
I'm afraid not.

Billy can't resist asking:

Any particular reason why not?

The driver shrugs and smiles:

No need.

Billy's confused:

But how's someone supposed ta find their way around if there ain't any signs?

The driver smiles again as if the reason's plain as day:

Because we all grew up here. We know our way around!

Billy tries to run that logic in his head, but then gives up and shows the driver Mira's address:

Then could ya take me ta here?

The driver checks the address, but then shakes his head:

Sorry.

Why not?

I'm not from around here.

As Billy tries to make sense, the driver points to another driver:

But he is!

Minutes later, another Rickshaw's driving Billy through more of Goa's lush countryside. After some time he pulls over:

This it? We here?

The driver, climbing out, calls back:

I just need to check on something.

As Billy looks on confused, the driver flags down a passing bicyclist and asks him directions in Hindi. The bicyclist, in turn, flags down a passing car. As the driver and the bicyclist consult the car's driver, a passing woman balancing a bowl on her head joins in the discussion as a truck driver, seeing the conference, slows to volunteer his expertise.

Pretty soon it looks like a mini convention, as quaint as it is amazing to Billy to see how many people stop by to join in the discussion, ready to help a stranger.

A crack of thunder overhead signals a sudden break and the convention finally breaks up. The Rickshaw driver comes back over, armed with a better sense of where to go.

He smiles back at Billy as if this is all in a day's work, fires up the Rickshaw, and speeds up, as the rain continues, drenching Billy and his driver.

Mira's lying on her bed, listening to the monsoon rains fall in buckets, feeling again as if she's drowning in an ocean of expectations and familial duties, when she suddenly hears a knock, startling her:

Not now.

Elie calls through Mira's door:

Some man wants to see you.

Mira grimaces:

Some man?

A white man.

I don't know any white men. Probably just some…I don't know. Tell him I'm not here.

As Elie moves off, Mira grumbles:

60

Who in their right mind would be out in this weather anyway?

As the rain continues to pour down, Elie cracks open the door to Billy standing there drenched, looking pitiful:
Sorry, but she's not here.
Do ya know when she will be in?
Elie, panicking, shakes her head and quickly shuts the door.
Billy considers knocking again but thinks better, shoulders his bags, and trudges back out into the downpour, not sure what the heck to do now. So he starts off down the street, looking for he doesn't know what.

As Mira lies there, she hears Elie passing by her door again:
Elie?
Elie opens Mira's bedroom door and leans in. Mira asks:
So who was it?
Elie shrugs:
Just some man.
Did he say what he wanted?
Elie shrugs again:
He wanted to know when you'd be home.
And what did you say?
I said I didn't know.
Mira considers it:
Was he selling something?
I don't know. Hats, maybe.
Hats?
Elie uses her hands to illustrate the shape of his hat:
It was like in those American movies?
Which American movies?
The ones Americans wear when they ride horses around and shoot people.
Mira's face fills with a slow-motion guffaw.

Moments later, Mira rushes out into the rainstorm, looks both ways to no avail, and then, guessing, races off down the road into the swirling wind and heavy rains.
As she hurries along in the dark, looking about, having trouble seeing in the dark and storm, she suddenly spots a lonely figure ahead...in a cowboy hat, and she feels her heart nearly explode:
Billy...Billy?
But Billy can't hear her through gusting winds and keeps walking.
So Mira charges after him, running, soaked, but narrowing the distance, calling to him, until he thinks he hears something in the storm and looks around, and then hears:

Billy!

His faced electrifies as he turns around and around, trying to see her in the storm, until he makes out her shape running towards him, and hobbles towards her:

Mira?

Billy!

As they rush into each other's arms, he drops his bags to catch her as she runs and leaps into his arms, squeezing each other as if their wily hearts had finally found a home…until Mira, just as quickly, pulls back, suddenly self-conscious, back-pedaling, trying to reestablish some already-abandoned boundary between them, as his rain-soaked, matted shirt and her drenched dress are making it appear they are already naked.

Realizing that her breast is plain to see through the wet, thin cotton, she quickly tries to scrunch the material to herself as he looks on, still reeling from her quick withdrawal:

What are you doing here, Billy?

He shrugs:

Ya said I should see Goa. So, here I am. Although I think I may have just given my Rickshaw driver a hundred dollar tip.

Mira has to laugh, despite her efforts to gain some perspective as Billy looks at her:

Anyway, guess I just felt I didn't say all I shoulda the day ya left, so…

As the rains continue to pound them she continues:

So you could have called.

Billy plays along:

Damn. Guess I coulda.

Mira eyes him, getting filled with a joy that also triggers her deepest fears:

Come on, let's get you out of this.

As Billy retrieves his bags, now flush with water:

Thought ya'd never ask.

Billy and Mira, dripping wet, are toweling off as Pita wheels in, followed by Manhar, Elie, Dilip and Alisha.

The family instinctively lines up as at a wedding reception, which Manhar notes, much to his dismay:

This is Billy Wilks, everyone…Billy, this is my mother, Pita.

Billy shakes Pita's hand, and Pita seems to take Billy in on a deep level, reacting to him intuitively.

Pleasure, ma'am. Your daughter was been most helpful ta me.

Mira jumps in to explain:

Billy was one of my best patients in America.

Billy smiles:

'Fraid I wasn't very patient, but she sure was.

62

Mira's family note, with varying reactions, the affectionate byplay between them. Mira tries to keep things moving by indicating Manhar, next in line:

And this is my father, Manhar.

Billy shakes his hand, suddenly feeling tongue-tied:

Sir.

Manhar eyes him suspiciously as Mira presses on:

And this is Elie, my sister…Her husband, Dilip, and my niece, Alisha.

As Billy shakes their hands, they continue to observe him as well as Mira, searching expectantly for any notes of romance, despite Mira's best efforts to make her relationship to Billy seem purely collegial.

Sorry ta barge in on ya'll like this.

They all check with each other, not sure what he means, so Mira translates:

He's saying he's sorry for dropping in unannounced like this.

They all immediately smile as if it was no problem – that is, except for Manhar, who thinks Billy may well be a big problem when it comes to his plans for Mira's life.

Elie then volunteers:

I didn't mean to be rude earlier.

Billy won't hear it:

Please. I shoulda called first.

Pita, meanwhile, is keeping a close eye on Billy as if she's reading his soul as Manhar tries to reestablish his kingdom by playing the host:

You must be tired from your journey.

Guess I am, a little.

Then you are welcome to rest here tonight, before you leave tomorrow for the rest of your journey.

Manhar indicates a hammock on their screened porch:

It's not much, but . . .

Looks like heaven ta me, sir.

As the others smile a little self-consciously, intrigued by Billy's arrival and Mira's tellingly controlled introductions, everyone moves off, leaving Pita to catch hold of Mira's passing hand and squeeze it as if to say "I know."

Mira delicately withdraws her hand, too apprehensive to even take in her mother's tacit approval. So Pita waves Billy over to whisper to him. As he leans in, she says:

Stay as long as you like, dear.

As Billy eyes her, surprised and pleased, but still worried what Manhar will think, Pita wheels herself off with a smile and a wave.

Later that night, as Manhar and Pita lie awake in the dark, Manhar speaks:

If he's one of her patients, why is he here? What, exactly, does he want? And most importantly, when is he leaving?

You all but told him to leave in the morning, dear.

Yes. I tried to, no thanks to you.

Pita pats Manhar lovingly on the stomach:

Get a good rest, dear. It could be a busy few days coming up.

Meanwhile, as Dilip and Elie lie awake in their bed, Elie mischievously tallies the evidence:

Long way to come for therapy, wouldn't you say?

Dilip shakes his head, knowing only too well what his wife's up to:

But then Mira was offering him "physical" therapy.

Don't start, woman.

I didn't start it. Mira did!

Dilip has to laugh:

Lord help him.

As Mira, wide awake, stares at the holes in her bedroom ceiling, Billy sleeps like a baby in the hammock, cradled in the palm of what feels like Karma, halfway across the world.

The next morning, Billy, an early riser like Manhar, finds Manhar in the kitchen, already preparing Pita's breakfast as Alisha slurps on some fresh cut mango at the table.

They both look up as Billy steps hesitantly in, and Manhar asserts, trying to take control:

Good morning.

Mornin'.

May I offer you some tea for your journey?

Please.

As Manhar stirs a pot of water, black tea leaves and milk, he sprinkles in some cardamom:

So, Mr. Wilks?

Billy.

How do you take your tea?

However be fine.

Manhar, finding Billy's lack of conviction about his tea, as grounds for even greater suspicion, adds a teaspoon of sugar on Billy's irresolute behalf.

He serves the tea, making something of a ceremony of his dutiful host-hood, and then gets back to making Pita's breakfast as an awkward silence hangs in the air.

Meanwhile Alisha's eyeing Billy, fascinated:

Are you a cow rustler?

No!

So, Mr. Wilks . . .

Billy.

What, exactly, brings you all the way to Goa?

Billy, hoping to lighten the atmosphere, tries:

Feels like Karma.

Manhar looks over with a disapproving confusion:

Karma?

Billy then tries:

Or maybe it's reincarceration.

Manhar winces:

You mean..."Reincarnation"?

Billy looks worried:

What'd I say?

I believe you said "reincarceration."

Billy's relieved:

Kinda the same deal, isn't it?

Before Manhar can respond, Mira thankfully sweeps in, worried to find Billy at the mercy of her dad:

Good morning.

Billy leaps to his feet, banging the table and nearly knocking over his tea in his eagerness to greet Mira, drawing a private scowl from Manhar as he does:

Mornin!

Later that day, as Billy and Mira walk in the humid air, Mira shoots a glance back at the house, worried what Manhar's thinking:

So what are you doing here, Billy?

Beats me. I asked that airline agent for a ticket ta Indiana. Next thing I know, here I am. Although, come ta think of it, maybe all that curry in the airplane food shoulda tipped me off.

Mira smiles, but she can't hide her concerns:

Things are different here, Billy.

Different how?

Mira stops, gathers herself and then says:

Guess as long as you're here...

She walks Billy into the Arpora street market – a crowded, narrow avenue lined with merchant booths draped in breath-taking hues of blue, pink, orange and creamy lemon yellow, or stocked with fresh fish, tropical fruits, vegetables, cashews and flies – where the well-heeled rub elbows with the bare-footed to haggle for their daily bread.

As they move into the throngs, Billy is alternately awed, moved, fascinated and chagrined by the breathtaking sweep of human experience weaving around them:

Whoa.

Mira notes his appreciation, and it inspires her:

There's more.

Mira leads Billy, blindfolded with Mira's scarf, out onto the white sands of Braga Beach, past the nestling coconut palms, down to the surf line:

May I present?

She then pulls the scarf away:

The Arabian Sea.

Billy stares at it, amazed and awestruck:

Holy Moses.

Billy yanks off his boots like a kid, rolls up his jeans as best he can and wades into the turquoise surf to feel its warm, soft waters. He moves around in it, speechless.

He then looks back at Mira, grateful beyond words as she can't help but smile, touched by his passionate appreciation, compelling her to hike up her dress and wade out into the surf with him as he shakes his head:

Unbelievable.

He looks back at the shore, wanting to see every view, turning his back on the surf, prompting Mira, who notes a coming wave, to get his attention:

Billy...Billy!

Billy turns just as a wave smacks into him, knocking him down, submerging him as it foams and swirls over him.

Mira, instantly horrified, rushes towards him, remembering he can't swim, only to see him lunge back up into view with a shout:

Yee-haw!

As he stands there dripping wet, exhilarated, she feels her pulse surge with delight.

So that's an ocean, huh? Well hot damn, I like the ocean!

He then watches in dumbfounded amazement as a water-buffalo, led to the surf by its owner, wades off into the water for a casual swim, taking a few laps beyond the breaking waves before calling it day:

Are ya kiddin' me? I'll bet ya anythin' Ray and Kooch ain't never seen anythin' like that! ...Holy crap.

As the sun turns red and gold, setting into the sea, Billy and Mira are strolling, along the tropical shoreline, letting the breeze dry their clothes. Billy looks over, filling his hungry eyes with Mira's beauty:

So ya think ya might ever consider comin' back?

Mira sobers. She knew this conversation was coming, and was dreading it.

I don't think so, Billy.

Billy slows to absorb that, feeling as if he just got punched.

I would have told you had you called.

Billy admits:

Maybe that's why I knew not ta call first.

As they stand there, at a turning point, feeling a soft sea breeze, Billy continues:

All my life, I've been tryin' ta make sense of things. Ya know?

She does know what he means, and nods.

And I thought I had finally made sense of my life, 'till you showed up.

Billy . . .

So ta answer your question, that's really why I'm here, Mira. Cause after you left, I realized that what I thought I knew, what I thought I'd figured out, didn't actually make any sense. And the only thing that did was you.

Mira, reeling, not knowing what to say, feeling as if anything she could say would only make things more confusing, finally takes his arm and turns him back towards town:

I have to get home now.

Back at the house, Billy, not sure what's going on, sees Mira, now dressed again in more professional attire, heading out:

I'll be back. I have to go...for a job interview.

She then sees Manhar looking on as if he's wondering why Billy's still around, so Mira artfully adds:

Dad, would you make us some of your world-famous Sheeth Kodi tonight? I wouldn't want Billy to miss out on it while he's here.

She then waves off and leaves, feeling ever more conflicted and flustered as Manhar looks back at Billy, realizing he's been temporarily out-maneuvered:

Of course. You'll need a good meal for your journey home, Mr. Wilks.

Please, it's Billy. Just...Billy.

Manhar is forced to accept, not exactly thrilled:
"Billy."

A half hour later, Mira's sitting in a medical clinic office, watching well heeled patients of all ages come and go, noting the success of the practice.

As she waits for her interview, she checks her watch, suddenly feeling sorely tempted to bolt. As she clouds over, fighting herself, a lean man in his thirties grandly moves into the room, wanting to impress. Maybe a little too much.

He walks to Mira holding out his hand with a big smile:
Mira! How are you?
Mira tries to rally to his enthusiasm.
Cammel, how are you?
Excellent. You look lovely, as always.
Thank you.

He graciously guides her into his private office, prominently featuring his expensively-framed medical diplomas:
May I get you something to drink?
No, thank you.
Cammel holds a chair for her and then glides around his oversized desk to take his seat:
So, how was it in America?
Interesting. Where I was —
Where was that?
In Texas.
Cammel smiles vaguely, not really sure where that is or what it means:
Anyway, it was...interesting.
Excellent.
His gaze lingers a bit too long, so Mira tries to move things along:
Anyway...
You haven't changed a bit.
Mira smiles courteously.
I, on the other hand, may look a bit different to you.
She can see how important it is to him that he seems different to her, somehow new and improved, even if he in truth looks almost abnormally the same. But she's too kind not to allow him his moment:
A little, yes. And it becomes you.
That's because things for me have changed. As your father may have mentioned, I've taken over the clinic from my dad.
And congratulations on that.

Thank you! I can barely keep up, what with all the new patients and responsibilities. Being successful is much more work than I ever would have imagined.

She smiles once more, allowing him this self-administered pat on the back.

But as an awkward silence threatens to follow, Cammel quickly fills the void with:

So, about the position: what I'm looking for, Mira, is someone I can work with closely, a "right-hand woman" if you will, who can turn my plans into reality, because I have plans, Mira. Really big plans.

Mira tries to formulate a response, taken off guard by the nature of the position.

Wow. I see. My dad didn't say anything, so I thought you might be looking for a physical therapist to fill in some hours.

Overshooting the mark, Cammel hears himself say:

I can always find a physical therapist. There are any number of qualified...

He catches himself, and turns a bit pale as he endeavors to dig himself out with:

What I'm really trying to say is I'm looking for someone with more of your unique talents...not that physical therapy doesn't take talent, because it does. A great deal of talent.

After Mira leaves, cordially promising to think about it seriously, Cammel paces his office, needing to calm his overheated nerves.

As the afternoon turns to evening, Mira steps out of the clinic and walks up the block, looking confused and troubled.

She knows this is a plumb offer, and one she'd be crazy not to take.

She also knows she feels like tearing her hair out, but not because of Cammel. And that only makes it more confusing because it would be much easier to be revolted or disgusted by Cammel. That would make the decision so much easier.

As she continues her walk home, what begins to trouble her even more is why she didn't jump on the offer immediately, not to mention why something in her gut is preventing her from sealing the deal in her mind, as if there was anything about the offer in need of consideration.

That night, as Elie sets the dinner table, she suddenly moves to retrieve a set of infrequently used silverware.

Over dinner, Billy notes them struggling to use the silverware, trying to keep up appearances as Manhar turns to Mira:

So how did your interview go?

Fine.

She knows Manhar is waiting for more:

Can I tell you about it later?

As Manhar nods, frustrated, Mira isn't announcing her new job. Elie jumps into the pause, offering her own conversational topic for consideration:

So how did you two meet?

Elie looks eagerly to Billy, compelling a response:

Well, after I got my legs broke in a car accident, Mira helped me get back on my feet. In more ways than one.

Elie, ever the romantic, marvels:

So if you hadn't been in the accident, you'd never have met?

Must've been my good "karma", huh?

Dilip looks over:

"Akarma".

Sorry?

When the good we do comes back to us, it's called "Akarma".

Billy smiles, appreciating the notion, but disagrees:

Can't think of anythin' I ever done good-enough ta deserve her.

As Elie melts, Manhar chokes and needs Mira to pat his back to clear his throat.

Dilip privately rolls his eyes at Elie and then tries to distract Manhar with:

So what do you think of my father in law's Sheeth Kodi? Really tasty, isn't it?

Billy smiles, hungrily taking a bite:

Real tasty.

Pita smiles, beginning to genuinely like Billy, especially because Billy tries to include Manhar in the compliment:

You and your daughter are excellent cooks, sir.

And that only makes things worse, because it prompts Manhar to look at Mira with a, "You cooked for him?" glare, even as the rest of the table beams up at her, with Alisha acting as their spokesperson when she inquires:

What did she cook for you?

Before Billy can answer Alisha, Mira interjects:

Muffins, which I burned pretty badly as I recall.

But then ya made me something just like this.

Elie's impish side can't resist asking:

Sheeth Kodi?!

I think so, yeah.

She made you Sheeth Kodi? So whose do you like better?!

Manhar, knowing only too well Elie's talent for stirring the proverbial pot, realizes he better wrest back control of this conversation, and so leans forward to ask:

70

So Mr. Wilks – Billy – where else in India will you be visiting on your trip?
Uh, really don't have any plans like that, as such.
So you came all this way to…
Thank your daughter for all she done for me in person, sir.

If Manhar had any doubts, or rather hopes, that Billy's intentions were strictly platonic, he now knows without question why Billy's here, which is why he then demands:

So when will you be going home?

A subtle chill frosts over the table, irking Elie and Pita, who find Manhar's approach boorish at best.

Monday, I guess, sir.

Manhar, having finally gotten a feeling that this will end, brightens and then tries to combat the looks he's now getting from Mira, Elie and Pita with:

Then we must all make sure Mr. Wills – Billy's – stay is as pleasant as possible until Monday.

Manhar nods back at Billy, trying to sandbag Billy into leaving Monday. Now the doorbell rings, drawing everyone's surprised attention.

Alisha, always up for a new adventure, jumps up before anyone else:

I'll get it!

As they wait for what Alisha will learn, an awkward silence hangs over the table, broken only by the sound of Cammel's voice echoing into the room as he follows Alisha into the dining area carrying a large fruit basket:

Mira feels the blood draining from her face as Cammel's cheeks, conversely, seem to be flush red:

I'm so sorry. I didn't mean to disturb your dinner.

Manhar beams as if his army has finally arrived to do battle:

Nonsense! Please, come in!

As Mira's stomach ties in knots, Cammel sees Billy, and instantly senses he may be competition. He then does his best to hide the surge of anxiety shooting up his spine and moves to extend his hand, feigning friendship:

My name's Cammel. Dr. Cammel Patel, Internal Medicine.
Billy shakes his hand, standing halfway up:
Billy Wilks. Ranch hand.
How do you do?

Cammel then turns to Elie and Dilip:

I just wanted to drop a little something off for the anniversary couple.

As Dilip stiffens, realizing he was well on his way to forgetting, Elie kicks him under the table:

How nice of you, Cammel? And to remember. So thoughtful.

Cammel smiles, but can't resist turning his attention back to Billy, compulsively driven to size him up:

So, what do you think of India?

Think I like it.

Cammel hears himself say:

Then perhaps you haven't seen enough of it.

As everyone looks around, reacting to that odd comment, Cammel hastens to get back on track by turning grandly to Manhar:

So, did she tell you about my offer?

Not yet.

Cammel, surprised, tries to play along:

Well I hope she doesn't keep you in suspense too long. Or me, for that matter.

Manhar shoots Mira a look:

Indeed.

Cammel then senses he best make a tactical retreat, and turns to the table:

Anyway, I'm sorry to have burst in on you all like this. Nice to meet you... Billy.

Billy. Happy anniversary to guys, and good night all!

Manhar hails him as he departs:

Good-night, Cammel. And do come again. Anytime. You're always welcome!

Cammel waves off with a special look at Mira, which Billy notes.

They then wait to hear the front door open and close again, at which Manhar turns to Mira:

I'd say your interview today went very well.

Alisha suddenly launches into an imitation of Cammel:

Because I love Mira, and I want to marry Mira. Please, Mira?

Sensing Billy deflating nearby, Mira snaps at Alisha:

Do you mind?

Alisha quickly falls silent, caught off guard, as Elie piles on:

Go to your room. That was entirely uncalled for.

But...!

No "buts", or I'll take away TV!

Alisha, feeling the injustice of the universe heavy on her back, trudges off as Mira, flustered, excuses herself, and goes upstairs, leaving Billy watching after her, shaken.

Later, as Mira washes Pita off from a wash bucket, Manhar steps in, looking as if he has something on his mind, but is having trouble expressing it. He finally kneels beside to address them:

So when are you going to accept Cammel's offer?

As Mira's eyes burn over at him, he leaves and Pita offers her daughter a compassionate gaze.

Still later, Mira tosses and turns in her bed, unable to sleep while Billy, suspended in the hammock, is fast asleep.

That is until Mira, tip-toeing up, kneels by him and whispers:

Billy?...Billy!

He suddenly startles awake, causing his hammock to flip him onto the floor with a hard thud:

Jesus…!

She winces, contrite.

Sorry.

As he climbs up, they discover a fresh cut over his eye, left from where his face hit the marble floor.

A moment later, they're in the bathroom; Mira dabs away the blood with a towel, nearly exploding with something to say, which Billy senses and whispers:

Go on, let's hear it.

My family thinks...

Billy waits.

That we're, you know, secretly together.

Billy considers it and then shrugs, taking it in stride as Mira boils over:

Did you ever think I might have my own plans?

He eyes her, confused:

I ain't tryin' ta get in the way of your plans, Mira.

No? Then why'd you come?! Why'd you just get on an airplane and come as if you owned the place?

Billy's lost:

Like I "owned the place"? I barely found your place.

But Mira isn't mollified, and she glares at him as if it's all his fault, confusing him even more:

I have a life here, Billy!

Ya mean with that doctor fella?

If you mean "Cammel", I've known him my whole life. I've only known you for what, a few months!

So?

Mira looks as if she might explode:

So?

Just then, they hear someone stirring in the house, and she instantly shushes him and then waits, worried they'll be discovered. She then flips off the bathroom light, leaving them in the dark, face to face.

When the sound stops, Mira leads him out into the balmy, tropical night.

Billy allows her to direct him, waiting until they're out of earshot of the house to ask:

So, you were sayin'?

So you have a girlfriend, Billy! Or a sorta girlfriend, whatever the hell that means!

He has to smile, which only frustrates her more:

Why are you smiling?

So ya were listenin', huh?

Damn right I was!

He sobers for her sake:

I told her Happy Trails, Mira.

She has no idea what that means.

Meanin' so long and adios.

She's still not sure what he means.

I told her good-bye, all right? Besides which, she wasn't even a sorta girlfriend in the first place.

Then why'd you say she was?

He takes a deep breath and exhales, admitting:

Pride.

"Pride"?

Guess I just…didn't wanna look lonely in front of you.

She takes note, despite her frustration, as he continues:

Lord knows I was already down on my luck. Throw in "lonely" on the deal, and I figured I wouldn't have had a chance.

She considers it and then balks:

But that's not really how it happened.

I know. But it wasn't until after ya'd left that I realized how I'd been feelin' all along, only I couldn't admit it to myself.

She tests him:

Why not?

He takes a moment, trying to decide how to explain before continuing:

Mira, me and my brother was raised in Foster care. And if there's one thing we learned early on, it's that ya can't depend on nobody. Or at least ya best not depend on anybody if ya wanna keep your heart in one piece…And I think ya know what I mean.

His eyes and words dive deeply into her, but she can't afford to admit it. Yet that doesn't stop her from wanting to know how he was freed from such a familiar fear, so she asks:

So what changed?

What changed; ya left, and I realized that my heart was broke; but unlike my legs, my heart, despite bein' broke, got right back up and kept right on goin'. 'Fact it led me all the way here, to you.

She eyes him, shaken, rattled, moved:
I don't need "Romeo and Juliet", Billy.
He waits for a moment and then smiles:
Think Cammel's gonna be disappointed ta hear that.
She rolls her eyes, exasperated:
He's not my boyfriend, all right?
He smiles slyly:
Does he know that?
She closes her eyes, feeling her original frustration boiling up again:
Don't you see? Anything I do, any choice I make, I'm disappointing somebody.
Failing somebody. And it usually ends up being me!...Why do you think I left here for
America in the first place?
For some of the same reasons why I came here.
She waits.
Ta know I didn't leave no stone un-turned, no trail un-taken when it came ta
the most important thing in my life. And for me that's you, Mira. That's you. And
it'll still be true even if ya turn me down.
She eyes him hard, deeply confused and conflicted.
Bill sees her struggle, and offers:
I didn't come ta make things harder on ya. I just...wanted ya to know that
meetin' ya is what made the man in me finally wanna stand up on his own two feet.
She stares at him, which he takes to be a "no" as he feels more
blood start to trickle from his eye. So he shrugs as if to say, I better attend
to this. As he starts back for the house, she stares after him, looking as if
she's going to explode, and then she calls after him:
Billy?!
He stops and turns to see her eyes burning into him.
She then starts towards him, gaining speed to suddenly lunge into
his arms and kiss him, smothering his lips, grabbing him as if she will
never let him go, only to just as suddenly push back from him and run off
into the night.
Billy stands there a moment, stunned. He then runs after her, trying
to find her.
But as he hustles through Arpora's empty streets to no avail, he
finally slows and gives up, realizing she's gone.

As Billy arrives back at the house, he enters to find Alisha, unable
to sleep, engrossed in late night black and white cowboy Western on TV.
Billy smiles, bemused by the Hollywood version of his life.
Ain't really like that.
Alisha looks up:
Can you ride a horse?
Since before I was born.

Alisha shakes her head, frustrated:
My momma won't let me ride one. Ever.
Why not?
Because of what happened to my grandma.
Billy sits down beside her:
Go on.
*She fell off a horse. Hurt her head. If Mira hadn't been riding with her, and
gotten her to the hospital, she would have died.*
As Alisha gets back to her movie, Billy's face fills with a new
revelation:
Good Lord.

As dawn shines through the window, Mira, having sneaked back
into the house, is asleep akimbo in her bed, until a sharp knock startles
her up:
Yes? What? Who is it?
She hears Billy ask from behind her door:
So where ya'll keep your horses?
I'm sleeping, Billy.
Not anymore, ya aren't. Now rise and shine!
What are you talking about?
Billy opens her door and leans in, uninvited:
Get up!
Mira gathers up her covers, trying to cover herself, at which Billy
has to smirk:
Now ya know how I felt.
Why do I have to get up?
Cause you and me got somethin' ta do. And I ain't leavin' here till we do.
Do what?

Mira, still groggy, is seated by Billy on a moving bus, looking the
worse for wear while Billy, conversely, looks positively chipper. He looks
over at her and shakes his head:
*Know why it would never have worked between us? Cause I'm a mornin'
person.*
She scowls back at him as the bus makes its way into the Goan
mountain wilds.

A half hour later Billy and Mira are standing outside a corral, eyeing
a mare:
Not bad. Not bad at all.
Billy climbs into the ring, and moves tenderly to the horse, talking
to it gently until it can accept his touch:

76

That-a-girl.

Billy then moves to a saddle perched on the corral, retrieves it, and lifts it onto the mare's back, saddling her up as Mira looks on, sensing trouble:

What are you doing?

Me? Nothin'. But you're goin' ridin'.

No, Billy, I'm not.

Mira, we gotta get your blood movin' ta where it can do some good.

What are you talking about?

I'm talkin' about movin' your blood from your head, where you're scared, ta your heart, where ya wanna ride this mare like the wind.

Mira is starting to turn pale as Billy offers:

Let me help ya with this, Mira.

I don't want to do it, Billy.

Billy reconsiders:

All right, then. But if ya ain't gonna not ride her, maybe ya could at least say hello?

Say hello?

Billy eyes Mira, challenging her:

I ain't gonna be here much longer, Mira. Humor me. Humor this mare.

Mira considers it and then rallies all her courage and climbs through the slats, but keeps her back against them as her heart starts to race, and she starts to climb back out:

Come, Mira. Ya made it this far. Time to get past some fear.

She considers, sorely tempted to exit the ring, but then turns back, wanting to finally do this. Billy smiles:

That a girl.

I'm not a girl!

I was talkin' ta the horse.

Mira winces.

Oh…So now what?

Now we'll just try ta do some breathin'. Ready?

She glares at him, but he continues, undaunted:

And deep breath in, hold it…and release. And again deep breath in, hold it…and release.

Mira can't believe she's doing this, but she definitely is doing it.

That's it. And again. Deep breath in, hold it…and release.

Billy then holds out his hand to her, inviting her to take it.

She galvanizes, warily. But Billy keeps his hand there until she can move close enough to put hers into his:

Keep breathin'.

Billy, like a bridge across a wide gulf, then draws Mira and the mare closer and closer, slowly and gently, until he can guide her hand into his.

He then places some sugar lumps on his palm, and the mare nibbles them from their combined palms as Mira looks down, her heart pounding, her eyes open wide with fear, but her hand still there to feed the mare.

Billy then helps guide her hand to stroke the mare's brow:

There ya go. So how about it?

How about what?

Billy indicates she should try sitting in the saddle.

No!

Why not? Ya can't go nowhere. And I'll be standin' right here.

You don't understand, Billy.

Wanna bet?

Some children's voices draw their attention, and they turn to see several boys donning Festival masks nearby.

The Monsoon Festival's next week.

Billy speculates wryly:

Ya sure they won't call it off on account of rain?

She makes a face even as she keeps a wary eye on the mare:

Funny, Billy. Very funny.

Not as funny as you comin' all this way, and not at least gettin' up there in a saddle again.

Mira eyes him, realizing he must know her history with horses.

How did you…?

Point is, if you don't do this now, with me here ta help, ya ain't never gonna get another chance. So what's it gonna be, Mira?

Mira sobers, considers his offer and then finds just enough courage to finally let him hoist her onto the horse and into the saddle.

Mira sits there frozen, unable to breathe.

Breathe!

Mira starts:

Right. Okay now what?

You tell me.

Mira hazards a quick glance around at the ring:

Maybe I should just sit here a moment.

You're the boss.

Billy then lets go of the reins, and starts back away:

What are you doing, Billy?

She's all yours now.

Why?

Just didn't want ya ta leave here thinking it was all me.

She shoots him a look, realizing he already knows her better than most.

Ya could even walk her around the ring, if ya felt like it. Or I could help.

Mira, her jaw tight, her muscles taut, nevertheless gives him a small nod, so small that he needs to double check with her:

Ya want me ta help?

She gives another quick nod and he steps forward and takes hold of the mare's harness.

Mira is tense, but determined:

Slowly.

Billy nods:

Slow it is.

He then looks at the mare:

Slowly. Got that?

He then gives a soft tug at the horse's harness, and they take a step.

Billy looks up at Mira for further instructions, and she nods, approving more.

So he gently tugs again, and the mare takes another step.

Maybe a few steps now in a row this time?

Billy starts slowly walking the mare around the ring, as Mira endures, trying to do her breathing exercises to calm her heart rate, slowly but surely finding her confidence...

Billy then releases the reins into her hands and backs away, smiling as Mira continues, circling the ring, amazed to find herself back on a horse.

Grows on ya, don't it?

Mira is able to smile for the first time today, and she looks over at Billy, starting to realize what he's done for her, until firecrackers suddenly begin to explode.

Billy whips around to see the boy in the masks setting them off and then hears a loud whinny and whips back around to see Mira's mare rear up and bolt out of the corral, knocking down the gate post meant to keep her in.

In an instant, Mira feels like a rag doll, holding on for dear life as the horse heads off onto a trail, as Billy helplessly shouts:

Mira!

He then looks around to see a rider walking a saddled horse back to the barn, and runs over, leaps on it and commandeers it away:

Sorry. Be right back!

Billy leaps on and gallops off in hot pursuit of Mira as she hangs on for dear life. The spooked mare charges forward, galloping at full tilt as Billy narrows the gap, compelling his mount to cut a better line, narrowing the distance quickly.

A few more bends in the trail and he manages to catch up to Mira as she struggles to keep from falling.

He then reaches over and grabs hold of the reins to yank back, pulling both their mounts to a rough and jerking stop.

As the horses finally come to a panting stop, he looks over at her, worried:

Ya okay!

She turns slowly, and he fully expects her rage, but then finds her face flush with an ecstatic joy:

Thank you! …Thank you!

Billy looks at her, utterly confused as she continues:

You have no idea. No idea!

Mira lunges to hug Billy, nearly falling between the two horses as she does, but Billy grabs hold of her, still stunned, to pull her back up.

That night, Dilip and Elie's anniversary party is in full swing, alive with traditional foods and dress, as well as the beat Abba, a Goan favorite.

A buffet includes spicy culinary favorites such as Sorputtyl, Vindaloo, Xacuti and Ambot Tik...

Billy, wearing a Kurta, one of those long, Nehru-collar shirts from Dilip's closet, looks on, appreciating the fun as Dilip walks up, a little drunk:

We'll make an honorary Goan of you yet.

Thanks for the shirt. I feel like I fit in.

That's the good thing about India: everybody fits in.

They then see Mira entering the room, dazzling in a breath-taking turquoise Sari.

Billy's jaw nearly drops from his skull.

Dilip grins knowingly over at him, encouraging Billy to go to her. So Billy takes a deep breath and moves through the guests to arrive at her side:

How do, ma'am?

Mira turns, and immediately smiles at Billy's Nehru shirt:

From Dilip.

Mira beams, seeing Billy as never before:

You look…good.

You look…beyond any words I can think of.

She smiles, touched, but then sees Cammel arriving at the party.

She sobers and Billy looks to see Cammel approaching, shattering this moment.

But before Cammel can make it across the room, Elie sweeps in to take Billy with her:

Want you to try something!

As Billy looks at her, stunned she would do such a thing, Elie whispers:

Trust me!

She takes him to the side of the room as the guests stream onto the dance floor, including Mira, now being led onto it by Cammel.

Billy winces, rocked by pain as Elie, still holding onto him, sympathizes:

You got it bad.

Worse than bad.

Elie smiles:

Good.

No, that ain't good.

Elie looks at him:

Feeling like you do is what it'll take.

Take to do what?

To let her know you're serious, Billy.

I came all this way, Elie. Ain't that serious enough?

It's a start.

He eyes her, curiously:

Meanin' what, exactly?

Meaning, Billy, if you really want her to spend her life with you, you better damn well be serious.

Billy considers it, taking her point to heart:

Yes, ma'am.

As they watch Mira and Cammel dance, Billy can't look and so turns away, prompting Elie to ask:

Do you dance?

Texas two-step, more or less.

Show me.

Billy looks at her incredulously:

Now?

Definitely now.

As Billy starts to show her, trying to catch the beat, Elie maneuvers them out onto the dance floor, where they quickly become the center of attention.

Soon all the Goan guests are trying their feet at the Texas two-step, including Mira and a very reluctant and uncomfortable Cammel.

As everyone starts to catch on, Elie deftly slides into Cammel's hands, nudging Mira into Billy's, who quickly dances her away.

Cammel looks on frustrated while trying to pretend he's happy to dance with Elie, who's smiling up to force his attentions.

A few more turns and Cammel, at his rope's end, finally begs off to watch Billy whirl Mira around, making it almost seem that this was his and Mira's anniversary party.

Late that night, as Billy packs his things, preparing to leave first thing in the morning, Mira walks into the room, now in pajamas.

Billy slows and looks up, feeling his heart thump in his chest as she struggles to say:

I just...

He waits, feeling as if his whole life hangs on just a word or two.

...wanted to thank you for coming, and not calling first.

Billy takes that in, trying to offer her his appreciation, too, even if his heart's breaking yet again:

You bet. Thanks for havin' me.

Can I get you anything?

Billy thinks:

Well, I'm all packed, so that's but...actually, there is one thing I wouldn't mind.

What's that?

Minutes later, Billy and Mira, laughing, run out onto the soft sands of Braga Beach in the moonlight to wade out into the playful waves, playing like children, then calming, recognizing in their look to each other the undeniable electric pull between, even as they recognize its ultimate impossibility...

A harsh ray of sun creeps onto Mira's face, blinding her as she tries to open her eyes. Irked, she rolls away to stretch, only to suddenly bolt up in bed, alarmed.

A moment later she runs to discover Manhar in the kitchen with Alisha, but no sign of Billy.

Where's Billy?

Manhar, knowing this will be hard for his daughter to hear, answers gently:

He left.

Left? Why didn't you wake me?!

He asked us not to.

Oh my... How long ago?

About a half hour.

A half hour?

Mira, panicking, charges out in her pajamas, grabbing her sandals on the way.

A half hour's rickshaw ride later, Mira finds herself anxiously rushing through Dabolim Airport, gathering odd looks as travelers notice she's wearing pajamas.

She crisscrosses the terminal several times before acknowledging she's too late, and that, despite all her rationality and sensible decision making capacity, she failed miserably to discern what she really wants, and that she has always found a way not to allow herself to have what she wants.

~*~

It's another hot, dry night in Dallas as Kooch waits outside the terminal, looking through the folks pouring out of the terminal. But as their ranks thin to only a few, Kooch frowns, worried that Billy didn't make it, until he hears:
Kooch.
Kooch turns to find Billy walking up behind him:
Where'd you come from?
India.
India, my ass.
Billy grins, admitting he's messing with Kooch, and Kooch shakes his head:
Damn fool. So where is she? You hidin' her, too?
It's just me, Kooch.
Kooch sobers, disappointed for Billy. So Billy tries to buck him up:
Come on, Kooch. Take me home.
I'm sorry, Billy.
So am I, Kooch. So am I.

As they speed along the highway, heading home, Billy looks out at the Texas evening:
So how's Ray been?
Been okay, I guess. Gone, mostly.
Gone where?
Some kinda business. You know Ray. Pretty much have ta sit on his chest ta get him to tell you anythin'.
Billy nods, conceding the point.
So will she ever be comin' back?
Mira?
Billy shakes his head:
Couldn't if she wanted ta. Not any time soon.
Why not?
On account of her Visa's expired.

Kooch shakes his head, sick at the thought:
Damn I'm sorry, Billy. She was a good one.
Billy nods, holding back his tears.
Yup.

After the long drive back to the Silver C Ranch Billy's shaken to see Ray sitting outside his trailer nursing a beer as Kooch pulls up.

As they pull closer, Ray stands to see if Mira's with them, but quickly sees she's not and so he plays it cool, well aware of the sting Billy must be feeling.

Billy climbs out:
Hey.
Hey.
Beer?
Can't toast ya without one.

Ray peels off a couple of beers from a six pack and deftly knocks off their caps, handing one to Billy and the other to Kooch. They all clink bottlenecks in a toast:
Welcome home, Billy.
It's good ta be home, fellas.

They share a look and take their swigs, not needing more than a look to say it all.

The next day, Billy's sitting in Ray's truck, traveling down the highway again.
So where we goin'?
Time ta take care of some business that's waited too long.
And what business would that be?

Two hours later, Billy and Ray are at a pay phone in a strip mall. As Ray looks through a white page, Billy looks around:
So this is Arroyo, huh?
Ray locates what he's been looking for.
There she is. Tiffany Parks.
And who's that?
Dodger's blonde friend.
Ray then jots down the address.

As the afternoon drags on, Ray and Billy pull up outside Tiffany's condo.

As Billy climbs out, Ray offers:
I could come with ya.
Thanks, but, no.

Billy then crosses the street, finds her condo door, and knocks, waits and then knocks again.

Dodger, looking sickly and paranoid, cracks it open, gets shocked at the sight of Billy, and quickly shuts it again:

I ain't goin' anywhere, Dodger. So ya might as well talk ta me. Unless ya want your neighbors ta know our business.

A moment later, Dodger begrudgingly cracks open the door, allowing Billy in.

Billy enters carefully, noting Dodger's disheveled appearance:

What the heck happened ta ya?

Never mind that. How'd ya find me?

Why'd I have ta find ya, Dodger?

What do ya want?

My money.

Yeah, well, I don't have your money.

Why not?

Cause it's gone.

Gone where?

Dodger shakes his head as if Billy couldn't possibly understand:

I used it ta leverage a position, okay?

A "position"?

In the stock market. Only it didn't work out.

Meanin'?

Meanin' the money's gone, Billy. All gone.

Just like that?

Just like that.

Billy eyes him incredulously:

Ya said ya'd transfer it, Dodger. That's what ya said.

Guess you can't believe everythin' you hear, can ya?

Billy feels his pulse quicken, his adrenaline pumping:

'Nother words, ya lied ta me, Dodger. In fact, ya been lyin' the whole time.

Dodger sneers:

Ah grow up, Billy. Welcome to the way the world works.

Billy feels an urge to punch Dodger, but he rides out the feeling long enough not to. Instead, he shakes his head, feeling the ties to his brother breaking as he looks up and says:

Naw, Dodger, this is just how you try ta work the world…And as far as I can tell, it ain't exactly workin' out for you, now is it? By the way, that check I gave ya; I closed that account.

As if on cue, Tiffany walks out of a back bedroom to see Billy:

What's that shit-kickin' brother of your doin' in my house?

Billy looks calmly back at Dodger:

Looks like your fast food ate you.

With a knowing, last look, Billy heads out as Tiffany says to Dodger one more time:

I don't want that lowlife hand comin' in here ever again, you understand?

A minute later, Billy crosses the street and climbs back into Ray's rented truck. Ray looks over:

So?

Billy shakes his head "no", at which Ray shrugs, bemused:

All that talk ya hear 'bout family values, most of it's just talk.

He starts up the truck:

Far as I'm concerned, family is as family does.

As they race back home, crossing the wide expanses of Texas, Ray suddenly slows and pulls up. Billy looks around:

Where we headed, Ray?

For one thing, we're takin' ya job-huntin'.

Something happen ta my job at the Silver C while I was away?

No.

So why're we goin' job huntin'?

You'll see.

They pull to a rundown barn with attached stalls, but overlooking a nice stretch of land.

Ray parks, and they climb out to have a look around, priming Billy's curiosity:

What is this place?

Ray demurs:

What do ya think of it?

Billy takes a moment to assess before replying:

Gonna need some work, but it's definitely got potential. And a nice slice of land ta go with it, too.

That it does.

Billy looks back over at Ray:

So what's the job?

Ray takes a moment and then says:

Came ta some decisions while you were away.

Billy waits.

Decided ta call it quits where the Silver C's concerned.

Billy looks over shocked, stung, feeling as if he's losing Ray:

You're kiddin'.

I better not be if I plan on goin' inta business for myself, which I do. And which is why I bought this place.

Billy's shock is back, but now because he's excited:

You're kiddin'!

'Fraid not. I figure a stable business is as stable as it gets these days, and Lord knows I know what ta do, so if ya know anybody who's good with horses, I might just have some work for him.

Ray keeps his eyes on the land, wryly allowing Billy a beat to realize what this means:

For real?

Couldn't pay ya much ta start, but then, you're used ta workin' hard for shitty pay.

Billy's eyes fire to life, reborn as he imagines a new life:

But ta make it worth your while, when I'm gone, I want you an April ta share it.

Billy starts again:

April?

Seein' the way ya went all the way ta India for love made me think...Anyway, Dodger may be your blood, Billy, but you're family ta me.

Billy feels his eyes misting, and rubs a rough wrist over them:

You're the only family I got now, Ray.

They hug.

Billy then looks around again at this place, excited by the possibilities:

We can do this!

He then looks around at Ray and comes out with a question:

So what are ya gonna call this place?

I was kinda thinkin' "The Golden Ray Ranch".

Billy agrees immediately:

Damn that's perfect.

Cammel is showing Mira around the clinic, introducing her to the staff and describing all its intricacies and services. She dutifully pays attention, looking positively pale.

~*~

Meanwhile, Billy spends his day working at the Golden Ray Ranch, mending fences, repairing stables, filling stalls with hay and welcoming families arriving with their horses, looking for a place to safely board them.

A few week pass, and Billy's life settles back into a routine of chores and errands.

One day, he stops by a Five & Dime to pick up some beef jerky, and sees Dodger come in. Dodger, true to his name, sees Billy and soon dodges away behind an aisle of pop tarts.

Billy takes a moment, goes over and finds him. Dodger looks up as if nicely surprised:

Hey.

Hey. Just wanted ta say take care of yourself, Dodger, and happy trails. And I mean that.

Billy then tips his hat, and heads out of the store, starting to feel fresh and free like a morning breeze as he climbs back into his truck and drives away on his way.

A half hour later, he passes under a new trellis, scripted with, "The Golden Ray Ranch", and drives up the road to the ranch house.

Billy parks, climbs out and walks to the main house to hear Ray plucking a guitar.

When Billy steps inside he finds Ray serenading April.

She beams over as Billy enters:

Hey, Billy.

Hey there.

Billy shoots Ray a grin, listens for a few bars and then heads back out as April and Ray trade a certain look.

Minutes later, he canters off into the hills to check on a fence post, which he sets right and secures with a few rocks.

He then climbs back on his mount to look out over the Golden Ray ranch – a Foster kid who finally feels as though he's home.

As he sits there, taking it all in, watching the sunset turn the skies red and gold, he sees dust trail rising from a distance, and makes it out to be a rider and mount galloping across the Golden Ray, angling towards him.

Billy's first instinct is to wonder who this person is on Ray's ranch, but as the rider and horse draw near, he begins to see it's a woman rider, with long black hair flowing behind her as she drives her mare onwards, drawing nearer and nearer until Billy's jaw suddenly drops open as his eyes and heart burn to life.

Mira, reining in her mount, trots the last few steps between them until she's by his side. They eye each other, burning with emotion. Billy stares back, thunderstruck:

How'd ya…?

Come back? Ray called me to make sure I could. In time, though, I'm guessin' I might just be single woman again, in case you're still interested.

"Interested"? Naw.

Billy adjusts his hat matter-of-factly as she looks on, momentarily thrown down, until he adds:

More like head-over-heels, 'turn-me-over-cause-I'm-crispy-done in love with ya, Mira. You, and your little bastard muffins.

Tears burst from her eyes as she climbs from her horse onto his to kiss him, now face to face in the saddle, to Billy's continued, glowing astonishment:

So changed your mind?

Guess I finally got my blood moving, from my head to my heart.

Her eyes mist, as do his:

Know whatcha mean.

Part of my life will always be in Goa, Billy.

Billy shrugs:

That's what airplanes are for.

She tears up all the more:

You sure we can make this work?

Think we already are.

They lean into kiss, each feeling as if for the first time.

Then Billy remembers something:

Well hot-damn, ma'am. And ya can ride, too!

Better than you.

Billy eyes her with mock indignation:

Pardon me?

You heard me, Cowboy.

He smiles as he responds:

If I didn't know better, I'd say that sounded like a challenge.

With her tongue firmly in her cheek, she shrugs:

Not for me. Maybe for you, of course. But a challenge? Not for me.

Billy's mouth creases into a glinting grin:

That a fact.

If you would help a lady back onto her horse, I'll show you.

He does help her. But as she settles back into her own saddle, she suddenly stares off behind him as if she sees something terrible:

What's that?!

The moment Billy instinctively turns to see what she means, he hears "Yah!" and turns back around to see Mira galloping off...

He smiles to himself, his head still spinning with it all as he mutters to himself:

Looks like ya got your hands full there, Billy!

He then cries "yah" and gallops off after her in hot pursuit – the two of them, riders against the wind, laughing as they trail clouds of joy against a cathedral sky.

~*~

Raised in Los Angeles, Darryl Sollerh's recent works include
"SHaDOW GAME", a Reader Views FIRS PLACE AWARD
winner, as well as "EDDY FALLS", "TRANCER",
"MINDFALL" and "ALIBIS OF THE HEART", a Readers'
Favorite Book Award FINALIST. All are now available in print,
as well as on Kindle, iPad, Nook and eReaders everywhere. For
more, visit www.DarrylSollerh.com.

~*~

For Nuriat, my love and wife

~*~